D0498388

UNLEASHED

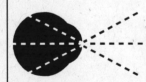

This Large Print Book carries the
Seal of Approval of N.A.V.H.

UNLEASHED

DAVID ROSENFELT

THORNDIKE PRESS
A part of Gale, Cengage Learning

GALE
CENGAGE Learning·

Detroit • New York • San Francisco • New Haven, Conn • Waterville, Maine • London

GALE
CENGAGE Learning®

Copyright © 2013 by Tara Productions, Inc.
An Andy Carpenter Mystery
Thorndike Press, a part of Gale, Cengage Learning.

Thorndike Press® Large Print Core.
The text of this Large Print edition is unabridged.
Other aspects of the book may vary from the original edition.
Set in 16 pt. Plantin.

LIBRARY OF CONGRESS CATALOGING-IN-PUBLICATION DATA

Rosenfelt, David.
    Unleashed / by David Rosenfelt. — Large print edition.
      pages ; cm. — (An Andy Carpenter mystery) (Thorndike Press large print core)
      ISBN 978-1-4104-6353-1 (hardcover) — ISBN 1-4104-6353-2 (hardcover) 1. Carpenter, Andy (Fictitious character)—Fiction. 2. Attorneys—Fiction. 3. Murder—Investigation—Fiction. 4. Large type books. I. Title.
PS3618.O838U55 2013b
813'.6—dc23   2013026625

Published in 2013 by arrangement with St. Martin's Press, LLC.

Printed in Mexico
1 2 3 4 5 6 7 17 16 15 14 13

This book is dedicated to Joanne and Doug Burns, two great friends who we met through Andy Carpenter.

In fact, Doug taught Andy everything he knows.

The three vehicles provided a surprisingly stable ride. The countryside in this desolate area of the world was rugged, famously so, but the cars were all-terrain models and could handle much worse. Besides, the ride would last half an hour maximum, and the passengers were not exactly unfamiliar with hardship and Spartan conditions.

Altogether there were eight men in the cars, three in the one in front, three in back, and two in the center car. Seven of the eight men were of little consequence in the grand scheme of things; they were there as protectors for one of the men in the middle car.

His name was Aarif Sajadi, and he was the target.

The aircraft flew twenty-one thousand feet above them, and they could neither hear nor see it. There were no passengers on board the flight; there never were. No flight attendants, no carry-on baggage compartments, no tray tables to be stowed, not even any seats to be restored to their original upright positions.

The pilot, Sergeant Brian Cole, could see the cars clearly, but even if the men stopped, took out incredibly powerful telescopes, and peered upward, they could not have seen him. That's because they were in the mountainous region of Pakistan, near the Afghanistan border, and he was sitting in a room at MacDill Air Force Base in Florida, drinking coffee and nibbling on a blueberry muffin.

The aircraft that Cole was piloting was a MQ-1B Predator drone. Many people thought of drones almost as small model airplanes, carrying cameras and functioning as eyes in the skies. But this one was twenty-seven feet long, had a wingspan of fifty-five feet, and weighed almost fifteen hundred pounds, including its two Hellfire missiles.

Cole was literally flying it with the use of a console and joystick, as if he were playing a video game. He tried to fully concentrate, as his training dictated, but it wasn't easy. He'd had a fight with his wife that morning before coming to work, and it was weighing on his mind. He thought maybe, when he was finished, that he should send her flowers.

Fortunately for Brian, though less so for the men in the cars, the Predator's MTS, or Multi-Spectral Targeting System, was doing most of the important work. Through the use of lasers, it had already homed in on the target and told the missiles where to go. All Cole would have to do was tell them when, by pressing a button.

At this point, the cars' passengers were lucky to be blissfully unaware. Were they suddenly to know of the aircraft and its intentions, there was nothing they could have done about it. The nearest cover was too far for them to reach in the little time available to them.

They were dead men driving.

Cole did not think much about the political or legal implications of what he was about to do. He knew he was functioning as part of the American government's strategy of targeted killings, and he certainly assumed that the target in this case was considered a terrorist bent on inflicting harm to the United States.

And that was absolutely true.

Cole was forever seeing claims in the media that the number-three person in the terrorist network had been killed; probably fifteen "number threes" had bitten the dust in the past year. Cole had no idea how many of those killings he had been responsible for, if any, but there was one thing he knew for sure: If he ever became a terrorist and reached number four in the chain of command, he wouldn't want to get promoted.

A final systems check was accomplished, Cole pressed the button, and the three cars, as well as their occupants, ceased to exist. For Cole, having been at this for a while, it was business as usual.

But what he did not know was that Aarif Sajadi was not like any other target. If Sajadi did not die instantly, then in his last moments he likely took some comfort in the fact that he had already plotted his revenge against his killers, halfway around the world.

His death did nothing to change that.

I, Andy Carpenter, am not often stunned. I'm a criminal defense attorney, and I've handled some high-profile cases with many twists and turns, so I've generally learned to go with the flow, to expect the unexpected.

I am therefore difficult to surprise, but at 7:34 P.M. on March 17, in my Paterson, New Jersey, office, I have just seen something that has left me shaken to the core.

Edna.

I used to think of Edna as my secretary, until she informed me she was my "administrative assistant." Then, a couple of years ago, she self-elevated her status to "office manager." She most often "manages" the office from a remote location, since she works maybe one day a week.

Actually, I've overstated it. She comes in one day a week, but she gets almost no work done even then. Instead she endlessly does crossword puzzles and considers herself the

11

best in the world at it. She also talks on the phone a great deal, mostly with her enormous extended family.

But to see her here in the evening, outside of business hours, is disorienting. Edna simply does not work overtime. She doesn't even work regular time.

In fact, it's more than disorienting; it's astonishing. It would be like walking into a bowling alley and seeing the queen of England throwing practice balls on lane fourteen. Yet here Edna is, hunched over her desk, writing on some papers, so engrossed that she barely looks up when I arrive.

With her is Sam Willis, my accountant, who has an office down the hall. He's sitting on a couch, but Edna's not paying any attention to him; she's too intent on what she's doing. Sam's the reason I'm here. He said he wanted to talk with me about something important.

"Hey, Sam . . . Edna," I say, which is a witty opening conversational gambit I've recently come up with.

"Andy, thanks for coming in," Sam says, while Edna merely manages an "mmm," without looking up.

I tell Sam to come into my office so we can talk. Once we get in there, I close the door and say, "It's seven thirty, and Edna's here."

"So?"

"So did we turn the clocks back or something, and I didn't realize it?"

He shakes his head. "No, but even that would be just an hour. She'd still be here late."

"I meant, did we turn the clocks back to 1978?"

"It's tournament time," he says. "She's been practicing."

"Aaahh." Suddenly it all makes sense. Edna has long been talking about entering a national crossword puzzle tournament, held once a year in Brooklyn. She's never actually entered, and I've always assumed it was due to some secret self-doubt about her prowess. But now she seems to be ready to throw her pencil in the ring.

"I don't think you're going to get much work out of her these next few weeks," Sam says.

"That's a shocker. What did you want to talk to me about?"

"Well, I think I may have a new client for you."

Sam says that with an expression and tone in his voice that indicate he thinks he is giving me good news. "Yippee skippee," I say.

I have a lot of money, many millions, some earned and more inherited. What I don't have is a desire to work. I'm not sure where I left it, but it's been missing for a while, and I haven't searched real hard.

Unfortunately, even though I don't seek clients, I seem to wind up with some, and long trials have often been the result. Working long trials is the only thing I dislike more than working short trials.

"You aren't interested in new clients?" Sam asks.

"What tipped you off?"

"Okay. Whatever you say." Sam seems rather chagrined at my reaction. He thought he was doing something good for a friend, and the friend just blew him off. I decide to soften the blow by acting half interested.

"What's the case? Maybe I can recommend someone."

He shrugs. "I'm not sure. I went to high school with this guy, Barry Price. Last time I had seen him was a couple of years ago, at the reunion. I think I told you about him; he's the guy who married my high school sweetheart, Denise."

"How come you didn't?"

"Believe it or not, I dumped her when I went off to college. Biggest mistake of my life."

"Sorry to hear that." Coming here is now showing signs of being one of the biggest mistakes of my life. This is already a long story, and Laurie Collins is waiting for me at home. That means that no matter what Sam was telling me, I'd want him to hurry the hell up.

"Anyway, he calls me the other day and invites me to a party at his house last night; you should see this place. I'm not sure why he invited me, but as I'm leaving, he asks if I can come back tonight, that he needs my help. He sounded a little worried about something, but he wouldn't tell me what. Then he asked if I still knew you."

"How did he know that?"

"I guess I mentioned you at the reunion, sort of name-dropping, you know? You're famous. He said he might want to hire you, and could I put the two of you together."

I've had a lot of high-profile cases over the years, many of which have been heavily covered in the media. But famous? Aww, shucks.

He continues. "He told me to pack a bag, that we'd be flying somewhere on his private plane. Barry's really rich, in case that changes your mind."

"Sorry, Sam. Not a chance."

"Really? I thought you might even come

15

out there with me tonight."

I shake my head. "I'm retired."

"Officially?"

I look at my watch and nod. "Effective seven forty-two P.M. But if you let me know what's going on, I'll recommend another lawyer."

"As good as you?" he asks.

"Don't be ridiculous."

Sam heads off to his friend's house, and I head home to Laurie. Edna remains at her desk, with no signs of leaving any time soon.

We have entered the bizarro world, where black is white, up is down, left is right, and Edna is in the office after five o'clock.

Like so many of these things, it began in a bar. Drew Keller was in the right place at the right time. And while an undercover cop's job was, in fact, to be in that right place at that right time, Drew had to admit to himself that this was more than a little lucky.

He was investigating a series of auto parts thefts in the Concord, New Hampshire, area, and had developed a relationship with a possible suspect whom he believed held some promise. The man's name was Rodney Larsen, and he was straight out of central casting for someone in Drew's line of work. Rodney was a walking undercover trifecta — stupid, talkative, and boastful.

Unfortunately, it's hard to reveal information that you don't have, and Drew was starting to believe that his instinct was wrong, that Rodney was a dry well when it came to the robberies.

And then he caught a possible break.

It took three nights and a whole bunch of beers, but Rodney said that his brother and another friend were going to "kill a big shot" and that he was a part of the team. He wouldn't say much more, but when Drew convinced him that he had access to high-tech weaponry and the willingness to use it, he was promised an invite to meet the others and possibly join the team.

So the plan was for them to come to the bar the next night to get to know Drew and see if he was suitable to sign up for whatever they had planned. He was there at midnight, and Rodney was waiting for him.

But the plan had changed.

Rodney's coconspirators had decided that they didn't think the meeting should be in public, so Rodney said that he and Drew were supposed to leave the bar and meet at their "place."

Because the original meeting was going to be in the public bar, Drew had not arranged for backup and surveillance. He was not comfortable heading into this situation, where he might be vulnerable, so he told Rodney that he would follow him in his car. That way he'd be able to call in for backup while he was on the way, and they could follow the GPS device that he would activate on his car.

But when they got to the parking lot, it all changed for the worse. Much worse. Rodney's brother Alex was waiting there, and he came up behind Drew and held a gun to his back. Then he took Drew's concealed weapon, forced him into Rodney's car, and they drove off together.

Drew was alone, and he was in trouble.

They drove to a service station about three miles away. The station was closed for the night, but the back room was open and occupied. Still at gunpoint, Drew was forced into that room, where two other men were waiting for them.

One of the men was Earl Raulston, the third member of the group. The other was a man the three conspirators knew only as Carter. They assumed it was a last name, but no one was really sure. What was obvious, however, even to Drew, was that Carter did not fit in with this crew and that he was in charge.

"Where is his gun?" were the first words out of Carter's mouth. Alex, obviously proud that he had been the one to confiscate it, rushed over to Carter to hand it to him. Carter looked in the chamber to confirm that it was loaded and then put it on the table.

"You are an undercover officer attempting to thwart our operation," Carter said.

"Hey, man, this is bullshit," was Drew's response. "Rodney here said there was some action to get in on, that's all. If you don't want me, that's cool."

Carter had no intention of arguing the point. Instead he took out his own gun and, without hesitating, shot Drew in the head, killing him instantly.

The others in the room were stunned, but no one was about to offer any criticism. "I knew he was dirty," Rodney said.

"This doesn't change anything, does it?" Alex asked.

"Actually, it changes everything," Carter said. He picked up Drew's gun from the desk, and in a devastatingly quick motion, shot the other three men with it.

He had the ability to have cleanly killed each with one bullet in the center of the forehead, but that's not how it would have gone down in a chaotic firefight. So now he fired more erratically, and in the case of Alex and Earl, used two shots to make the kill.

The three murders took fewer than five seconds, leaving Carter the only living person in the room. And he would be there for a while; this was a scene that would have to be choreographed.

What law enforcement would find would be implausible but not impossible. Which would be plenty good enough.

Sam Willis kept his glove compartment full. In addition to the registration, insurance card, and other documents that are found in most cars, he kept a substantial number of wrapped Weight Watchers Oatmeal Raisin Cookies. He found them surprisingly good, and even though they obviously weren't fattening, he was able to overcome that deficiency by inhaling up to ten at a time.

But when Sam was driving, the glove compartment was also an electronics warehouse. He kept his iPad, iPhone, and Black-Berry tucked away in there, which was essentially an act of self-preservation. Sam simply could not resist talking on the phone and texting while driving, so he protected himself from those unsafe activities by putting the devices out of reach.

That is why he had none of those distractions during his nighttime drive to Barry Price's house in Smoke Rise, New Jersey, about forty-five minutes from Paterson. Sam was cutting it pretty tight; with no traffic he'd get there at eight forty-five, which was when Barry told him to arrive.

Unfortunately, the forty-five-minute estimate did not take into account the accident on Route 23 that had traffic backed up for almost a mile. Sam's GPS, the one device that wasn't banished to the glove compartment, alerted him to the problem, and he got off the road to take back streets.

He found himself on a dark country road and basically had no idea where he was, but with his GPS he wasn't worried about getting lost. He was more concerned about being late and considered calling Barry, but that would have meant stopping to get the phone out, which would have just taken more time.

He heard the thump more than he felt it, but it jolted him. He had hit something, there was no question about that, but he had no idea what it was. It was most likely an animal, but in the darkness Sam couldn't be sure.

He had a momentary desire to just drive on, but he couldn't do it. He had to stop and find out what happened.

Sam pulled over but immediately realized that whatever he had hit was behind him, in an area where it was too dark for him to see. So he did a U-turn and crossed over to the other side of the road, angling the car so the headlights might light up the area he thought he needed to search.

He got out and walked toward the brush on the side of the road, and for about a minute, which seemed like an hour, couldn't find anything. Then he heard a noise. It was hard to tell exactly what the sound was, and he went toward it.

Sam was nervous; the noise seemed to be coming from the fairly heavy brush, and even with the car's lights, it was hard for him to see. If a wounded animal was lying there, it could be dangerous.

And then he saw it, lying immobile but with eyes that were awake and alert. In the deep brush it was hard to tell what it was, maybe a coyote or maybe a dog, but the message in its eyes was clear: *Help me.*

"Shit," Sam said and ran back to his car. He got in and pulled it up very close to the animal, so the lights would better brighten that particular area. He also turned on the hazard blinking lights, and then he got out his cell phone to call the police. It wasn't until after he dialed 911 that he realized there was insufficient cell service in the area.

Things were not going well, and to make

matters worse, it was starting to rain.

He debated whether or not to drive until he got cell service but decided not to. First, he wasn't sure that he'd be able to identify the location when he got back. Second, the animal was fairly close to the road, and there was a chance, albeit remote, that another car could drive over it.

So he stepped out into the road to flag down a passing car. In the steady rain it was somewhat dangerous, but the road wasn't curved there, so Sam felt that oncoming drivers would have enough time to see him.

Unfortunately, there weren't many cars, maybe one or two a minute. The first six cars passed him by, barely slowing to avoid him, but the seventh slowed to a stop. By then the rain was coming down hard.

He went to the passenger window, and when it opened he was surprised to see that the driver was a woman. She was at least sixty years old, and Sam wanted to tell her that she was nuts for stopping.

"Car trouble?" she asked.

He shook his head, which was by then soaked. "No, I hit an animal. It's alive, and I was trying to call the police, but there's no cell service."

"Oh . . ." she said, apparently upset on the animal's behalf. She took out her phone and looked at it. "I've got two bars. Let me try."

And she did just that. He heard her tell the dispatcher that she was on the Canyon Road, three miles south of Kinnelon. She asked Sam his name, and told them that Sam would be waiting for their arrival. His nod confirmed that he would in fact be doing just that.

When she got off the phone, she asked Sam if he wanted her to wait as well. The truth was that he did, because she seemed competent to handle anything that arose, but instead he thanked her profusely and sent her on her way.

She was barely out of sight when he realized he had made a stupid mistake. He should have asked to use her phone to alert Barry to what had happened and explain that he would be late.

It took almost fifteen minutes for the police to arrive, during which time the rain got even more intense. A single squad car pulled up, and two officers got out.

"You Sam Willis?" one of them asked. Before Sam could even respond, he asked, "Where's the dog?"

"I'm not sure it's a dog, but it's over here. And it's alive."

Sam led them to the spot, and the officers

shined a flashlight on the wounded and drenched animal. Sam saw it and said, "It's a dog."

The other officer frowned and said, "We'll take it from here."

"What are you going to do with it?" he asked, afraid that they might shoot it on the spot.

"There's an animal emergency hospital about two miles up the road. That's where it's going."

"Is there anything I can do?" Sam asked.

"No," he said, and then seemed to soften. "Don't worry about it, pal. It's dark here; you didn't do anything wrong."

The incident had left him shaken, and the look on the dog's face would stay with him for a while. Sam got back in his car. It was only about seven minutes from where he was to Barry's house, and rather than call he decided to just drive there.

It was an exclusive gated community, and a guard had to call Barry to get authorization for Sam to enter. Sam had gone through the same process the night before, at the party.

Each house in the development was impressive, and Barry's might have been the nicest of all. The previous night there had been valet parking for all the guests, but

27

when Sam pulled up this time, only Denise Price was there to greet him. Shielding herself from the rain with an umbrella, she went to the passenger window, and he lowered it.

"Hi, Sam. I'm sorry, but Barry asked me to tell you he couldn't wait any longer and that he'd call you tomorrow."

"Damn. There was traffic on the highway, so I got off the road and wound up hitting a dog."

"Oh, no."

"He's alive but hurt pretty bad. Anyway, please apologize to Barry for me."

"I'm sure he'll understand," she said. "Would you like to come in and dry off? Maybe have a cup of coffee?"

He laughed. "I don't think I'll ever be dry again. But coffee sounds good."

"Come on in." She looked in the back-seat. "Your seat is all wet." She opened the back door and wiped the seat down a bit.

"It's fine," he said. "The advantage of buying plastic."

She laughed and closed the door. Sam got out of the car, looked up into the driving rain, and asked, "Barry's flying in this?"

She nodded. "He's a very experienced flier."

"Good."

Mine is a simple life. I don't clutter it with rules, and I refuse to be bound by rigid preset routines.

Of course, there are certain things I do and others I don't do. I think that in the last televised NFL game that I missed, the players wore leather helmets. I will never turn off a *Seinfeld* or *Honeymooners* rerun, and if Daniel Day-Lewis is in a movie, I'm there opening day.

Conversely, I have never been to a ballet or an opera since someone was foolish enough to invent them, I will neither read a Russian novel nor eat their soup, and you couldn't strap me into a chair to watch a soccer game.

But there is one thing I do religiously, not because I'm obligated to but rather because it gives me immense enjoyment. I cannot remember the last day I didn't take a walk with my golden retriever, Tara.

I do it because I enjoy spending time alone with her; it clears my mind and lets me focus on that which is important. I also do it because she so obviously loves it, and it's a pleasure to watch her.

The only thing better than taking a walk, just Tara and me, is taking a walk, Tara, Laurie, and me. They are my two loves, and living under the same roof as them, and sharing walks with them, make every day the best one of my life. The only obvious exceptions to that are the two days that the Giants beat the Patriots in the Super Bowls.

Laurie and Tara are waiting for me on the front porch when I get home. It's only forty-five degrees and raining lightly, but they don't seem to mind. Within ten minutes we're ambling along in Eastside Park, near our home in Paterson.

Once we get in the park, we take Tara off the leash. The leash is a device that I find demeaning to her, and not using it lets her roam at her pleasure, always remaining within our sight.

The park is not well lit and is said to be dangerous at night, but I'm not worried because Laurie is with us. She's a former Paterson cop turned private investigator, and between her and Tara, I'm protected enough.

"Edna was working late tonight," I say.

"Excuse me?"

"Well, not exactly working. She was in the office until past seven thirty, preparing for a crossword puzzle tournament."

"Wow," she says. Then, "What were you doing in the office?"

"Sam has a friend he wants me to take on as a client."

She shakes her head in amazement. "Edna working late and you having a client. It's a strange world we live in."

"I told Sam no. I said I was retired."

She nods. "Order is restored."

"Maybe I should make it official. You know, close the office. That way I won't be tempted to work."

"Are you tempted now?"

"Not at all."

"The removal of nonexistent temptation doesn't seem like it should be a priority."

"But that way people would stop trying to lure me back in."

"What about Edna?"

"She'll be fine; I'll give her plenty of severance. And Hike has as much work as he wants." Hike is the lawyer who works with me on the rare occasions that we have a case.

She thinks about it for a moment. "Whatever makes you happy, Andy. It's not like you're working now anyway, so it won't change your day-to-day life. You can focus on the foundation."

"Right." She's talking about the Tara Foundation, a dog rescue operation that Willie Miller, a former client, and I are partners in.

"So what's the downside?"

"I'm not sure," I say, since for some reason I'm not.

"Let's talk about it when I get back."

She says it casually, but it feels like a two-by-four hitting me on the head, even though I'm not sure exactly what a two-by-four is. I know it's wood, but two feet by four feet? Two inches by four inches? Neither seems right.

I had forgotten that she was leaving to spend two weeks in her hometown of Findlay, Wisconsin. It is something I'm dreading, since the last time she went back there she wound up taking a job as the local police chief, and it split us up for six months. Those were six long months.

"Do you really need to go?"

"No, I don't need to, I want to," she says. "I want to remain connected to my friends there. You know that."

"It could snow."

She nods. "Yes, there's always that danger, scary as it is. So I'll bring boots, and maybe even gloves."

"When are you going?" I ask, even though I know the answer.

"Wednesday morning."

"I've got an idea; I meant to talk to you about it," I say. "Let's get married on Tuesday night. We've been putting it off long enough. And there's no Knicks game that night, which is God's way of telling me that it's the perfect time."

Laurie turns to Tara, who is busy sniffing her way through the park. "Tara, have you ever heard anything as beautiful as that?"

Tara doesn't say anything; she might well be too choked up to bark.

"It's every girl's dream, Andy, but it might be a little spontaneous for me. Forty-eight hours isn't much time to send out the invitations, rent the hall, plan the menu, get a dress . . . all that would take at least three days."

"Okay, you're absolutely right, forget the wedding. Been there, done that. Let's just go on a honeymoon instead. We'll go south where it's warm, lie on the beach, drink piña coladas with little umbrellas in them, do that thing where you sneak under that bar . . . what's that called?"

"Limbo."

"Right, limbo. I'm not sure if I told you, but I came in third in the state limbo finals in high school. I'll teach you how to do it."

"So not Wisconsin?" she asks.

"I'm not ruling it out, as long as they have sunny beaches, piña coladas, little umbrellas, and limbo."

"I don't think Wisconsin is going to work. They don't have any of that, especially in March," she said.

"I'm willing to be flexible," I say. "The little umbrellas are not a deal breaker."

"I'm going to Wisconsin, Andy. But I'm not going to stay there this time. I'm coming home to you."

"That's what you said last time."

She grabs my hand and says, "Come on. Let's go home and you can give me a going-away present."

Barry Price did very well for himself. Sam had already known that, but sitting in his home, he realized it then more than ever. The previous night at the party, the large crowd of people seemed to prevent him from getting the full scope of the place. It was spectacular.

So was Denise, who seemed to get better looking every time he saw her. Combined with smart and funny, as it was in her case, it formed a deadly combination. Being with her didn't seem weird at all; it was like they picked up right where they left off, but without the making-out part.

She seemed like she wanted to talk, and every time Sam mentioned something about leaving, she poured him another cup of coffee.

At one point, she said, "It's amazing how much time has passed, Sam. It's like we knew each other in another lifetime."

"You were the first girl I kissed," Sam said. "And I haven't gotten any better at it since."

She laughed. "I doubt that's true. And you taught me a lot."

"Like what?"

"Well, you taught me how to drink beer."

He smiled at the memory. "You were a quick learner."

She got up and went to the kitchen, but this time instead of coming back with more coffee, she brought two open bottles of beer. She handed him one, and they clicked bottles and toasted "old times."

There seemed to be a loneliness about her, but Sam could have been wrong about that. Judging women's feelings was not really his specialty.

A couple of times she made vague comments that led Sam to believe that all might not be perfect between her and Barry, which was far from a surprise.

The previous night at the party, they had a rather public argument. It was over something insignificant — Sam thought it was about which wineglasses Denise was using — but even though it was a brief flare-up, it was uncomfortable for the guests.

Altogether, Sam and Denise spent a couple of hours laughing about old times, which always seem a hell of a lot more fun than when they were new times.

It was close to eleven o'clock when Sam finally stood up to leave. A moment later the doorbell rang, and Denise looked worried. "Who could that be?" she asked to no one in particular. Then, "Must be a neighbor. I didn't buzz anyone through the gate."

Denise went to the door, and Sam was maybe twenty feet behind her. She opened it, and Sam thought he could see two men standing there, one in a suit and the other in a police uniform.

They were talking softly; Sam couldn't hear what they were saying. But suddenly Denise shrieked, a piercing sound that Sam instantly knew he would never forget. She then slumped to the floor, sobbing.

Sam ran to her and, along with the two men, helped her to her feet and onto the couch. "What happened?" Sam asked, more of the men than of Denise, who was crying uncontrollably.

The man in the suit answered, "Her husband's plane crashed."

"Oh, damn," Sam said. He wanted to ask if there was any chance that Barry had survived but didn't want to do so in front of Denise. In any event, based on her reaction to what they had told her, it seemed highly unlikely.

"Who are you?" the suit guy asked.

"I'm a friend of hers and her husband . . . of Barry. We grew up together."

"Do they have family nearby?"

Before Sam could answer, people started coming through the door. They must have been neighbors, and Sam figured they had heard Denise's scream. A total of seven people arrived, and it was left to Sam to tell them what had happened.

They immediately went to Denise to console her, though that seemed impossible at the moment.

Sam felt like he had no role to play there; he clearly was not as close to Denise as the people who had come in. The guy in the suit went over to Denise on the couch and tried unsuccessfully to talk to her. He finally gave his card to one of the neighbors and said something to them that Sam couldn't hear.

So Sam decided to leave, wishing he could do more but realizing that he couldn't. He got his coat from the hall closet and walked out without saying anything to anyone. As he got into his car, he saw that the two cops were leaving as well.

The mind sometimes works in strange ways. It wasn't until Sam was halfway home

that he realized he was supposed to have
been on that plane.

"Andy, I've got to talk to you." Through my sleep-induced haze, I recognize that it is Sam's voice.

"Sam, what time is it?"

"Six o'clock. I'm sorry, but I've been up all night."

The stress in his voice is obvious, and I half sit up on one elbow. I can see Laurie do the same. "What's wrong?" I ask.

"I almost died last night."

"Where are you?"

"I'm at your house," he says.

This is not making any sense. "What are you talking about? I'm at my house, and I don't see you anywhere."

"I'm in your living room. I didn't want to ring the bell and wake you up."

"I'll meet you downstairs," I say. "Thanks for not waking me up."

I quickly update Laurie on the phone conversation, throw on some clothes, and

40

go down to find out what's going on with Sam. He's sitting on the couch petting Tara, whose head is in his lap.

"You should lock your door," he says.

"Not necessary," I say, pointing to Tara, who seems annoyed that Sam has momentarily stopped petting her. "I've got a vicious guard dog."

Laurie comes down, and we go into the kitchen to get coffee. Sam tells us the entire story from the previous evening. It has clearly left him shaken, and I can't say that I blame him. Just hitting a dog would be enough to freak me out. But after that he had a friend die, and then a kind of near-death experience that would be the emotional icing on my cake.

I'm not quite sure why Sam is here this early in the morning; maybe he just needs someone to talk to, and he couldn't wait.

But that turns out not to be the case. "Andy, that dog saved my life."

"In a way."

"No, literally. If I hadn't hit him and stopped, I would have been on that plane."

"I guess that's true."

"Where is the dog now?" Laurie asks.

"At a vet's office near where it happened."

"How badly was he hurt?" I ask.

"Pretty bad. I'm not sure if he made it."

41

I already have the car keys in my hand. "Only one way to find out."

We drive out to where Sam thought the accident had taken place, though he couldn't be sure that he was right. "They said it was a couple of miles up this road," he says, so we head in that direction. Sure enough, it's on the left side, a small place called Williams Animal Hospital. A sign in the window advertises "Low-cost spaying and neutering," and another reveals that they have a twenty-four-hour emergency staff on the premises. That is no doubt why the police brought the dog here.

We go inside, and Sam explains to the receptionist that he had hit the dog, and we want to know its status. The young woman agreeably says that she will check with the veterinarian, and we wait while she goes in the back and does so.

The vet comes out to talk with us. He can't be more than thirty years old and identifies himself as Dr. Castle. "There was a golden retriever brought in here last night. I assume that's the dog you're talking about?"

"A golden retriever?" I ask, feeling like I just got kicked in the stomach. I love all dogs, but the idea of a golden lying by the side of a road in pain is absolutely horrifying.

Sam shrugs and says he has no idea what kind of dog it was; it was dark. "But I'll know if I see his eyes; they looked right through me."

The vet lets us go into the back and leads us to a dog lying peacefully on a blanket in a run, which is essentially a large cage. There is another blanket lying over him, concealing his back end. There's no doubt; it's a golden.

The dog is alert and staring at us, and I immediately know what Sam meant about his eyes. He doesn't move any part of his body; I don't know if he's unable to or not.

"That's him," Sam says. "No doubt about it."

"What's wrong with him?" I ask.

"I'm pretty confident he has a broken rear left leg," Dr. Castle says. "Other than that he seems to be in surprisingly good shape."

"So you're going to do surgery?" I ask.

Dr. Castle hesitates for a moment and then says, "I wouldn't think so."

"Why not?" asks Sam.

"He's not a young dog. Based on the condition of his teeth I would estimate he's six or seven years old. There were no tags on him and no identifying chip. In this condition, at this age, he's not likely to be adopted, so . . . if no one claims him I would think we would be instructed to euthanize him."

Sam had been leaning over and petting the dog, but when he hears this he jumps as if someone shoved a hot poker up his ass. "Are you out of your mind?" he yells.

"It's not my decision," Dr. Castle says, backing up a little.

"You're damn right it's not!"

It's a rare situation involving a dog's welfare that I'm the calm, rational one, but that's the role I assume here. I'm able to do that because there is no doubt that the end to this play has already been written. We are not leaving this place without this dog.

"We'll take the dog and pay for any charges you've incurred," I say.

Dr. Charles shakes his head. "I'm sorry, but the procedure is that we first have to wait five days for an owner to possibly claim him."

"So you'd let him lie there with a broken leg for five days?" Sam asks. "How would you like it if I tried that on you?"

I don't think I've ever seen Sam this upset.

"We're going to amend the procedure in this case," I say. "Here's what's going to happen. We'll take him, and if the owners show up, you can refer them to me. I'm an attorney; I'll leave my card with your receptionist."

"But —"

I cut him off. "If that doesn't work for you, you can report to the police that we stole him, and I'll tie you up with so many lawsuits and depositions, you'll want to self-euthanize. Are we clear?"

He doesn't respond "Crystal," but it turns out that we're so clear that he lends us a stretcher to take the poor dog out to my car. Goldens are remarkably stoic. If I was in the pain that he is probably in, I'd be calling for my mommy.

We take him to my vet in Paterson, who is also board-certified in surgery. He X-rays him and tells us that it is a significant break but one that can be repaired, and he will do so this afternoon.

On the way out we stop at the reception desk, and I tell Julie to put the charges on my account. Since this vet treats all of our foundation dogs, my account is roughly equivalent to the GDP of Bulgaria.

"No way, Andy," Sam says. "He's my dog; I'm paying."

"Does he have a name?" Julie asks.

Sam nods. "Crash."

Barry Price's death is a big media story. Certainly not Michael Jackson big or Princess Diana big or even Steve Jobs big, but it makes the evening newscasts. He was an important businessman, the principal owner of a hedge fund with many billions in assets. That, plus the fascination that the public always seems to have with plane crashes, has deemed it worthy by the media.

The circumstances are somewhat unusual. Price was a very experienced pilot, and his plane was modern and fully equipped. It had been serviced just that morning, with no problems found, though of course that doesn't preclude the possibility of mechanical failure.

There were no radio signals from Price indicating trouble, which led to some speculation that he might have had a heart attack or for some reason suddenly lost consciousness. The plane came down in some trees, actually bounced off them, and Price's body was thrown clear before the subsequent crash and explosion. That was fortunate for the investigation, if not for the pilot.

I haven't said anything to Sam, but I find it at least somewhat curious that a man died a violent death the day after he asked Sam if he could make a connection on his behalf to a criminal attorney. At the very least it's a coincidence, a phenomenon that I do not believe in.

Whatever the circumstances, Barry Price is forever on the list of people who will never be my clients.

Crash has come through the surgery well and is recuperating comfortably at the vet's office. I know this because Sam calls me pretty much every twenty minutes with updates. He must be driving the entire vet staff insane. Though Crash is immobile and hasn't left his dog run, he has already conclusively demonstrated to Sam that he is the smartest dog in America.

Today I'm working at the Tara Foundation building in Haledon, something I've been doing more frequently lately. Willie Miller and his wife Sondra have tradition-ally done 95 percent of the work here, and I'm trying to cut into that percentage at least a little bit.

We rescue dogs from local shelters and keep them in our facility until we can place them in good homes. We provide whatever vet care they need, and both Willie and Sondra make them feel loved. They are able to do that because they actually do love them. I am totally crazy about dogs, but compared to Willie and Sondra, I can take them or leave them.

"We got people coming in to look at Ripley. You want to sit in?" Willie asks.

He's referring to potential adopters coming to see an adorable two-year-old golden retriever mix named Ripley. The routine is that they spend time with the dog, make sure it's a good match, then answer some questions and fill out an application. Willie makes the final decision about adoptions, though he can be a little demanding at times.

Sondra brings in the Happels, Ryan and Tracy. Ryan is at least six six, which means he probably has fourteen inches on his wife. But the vibe that they give off says that Tracy is in charge, and she can barely conceal her excitement at the prospect of meeting Ripley.

"She looks so cute in the picture," Tracy gushes.

We put photos of all our available dogs on

our Web site, so she must have seen it there. Sondra says that she'll be right back with Ripley, and Tracy says, "Oh, I can't wait."

"Tracy's wanted a dog for a while," Ryan Happel confides. "I've been resisting."

Willie hasn't said a word, which is not a good sign. When Willie likes you, you can't shut him up, so I suspect he's not yet a fan of the Happels.

Sondra brings Ripley out, wagging her tail and looking happy at the chance to social- ize. Willie goes over to her and scratches her around the ears. "How's my little girl?" he says.

Tracy's enthusiasm level has obviously and immediately gone down. "This is Rip- ley?"

"In all her glory," I say.

"She's prettier in her picture," Tracy says, effectively ending any chance they have of getting Ripley or any other dog from us. "What do you think, honey?"

"Is she a purebred?" asks Ryan. Neither of them have petted Ripley or gone over to her, another adoption-killing move.

"She's a mix," I say as I turn my focus toward preventing Willie from slaughtering the unsuspecting Ryan. Willie loves these dogs and has no use for anyone who doesn't share those feelings.

"What's with her teeth?" Ryan asks. Ripley has a small space between two of her front teeth, which in my view increases her adorableness. Obviously Ryan doesn't see it that way.

"You want to find out what it's like to have spaces where you're supposed to have teeth?" Willie asks. Willie is a black belt in karate and in seconds could arrange for Ryan to be sucking all his meals through a straw for months.

"Willie . . ." Sondra says, knowing where this could be headed.

While Ryan may not be a good judge of dogs, he is a good judge of Willie, and he backs down quickly.

"I don't think Ripley is right for us," Ryan says.

"You got that right," Willie says.

I intervene and usher the Happels out. I don't make any apologies for Willie. On some level I'd like to be Willie, to feel no hesitation to say whatever I'm thinking.

When I leave the foundation, I stop at home to feed and walk Tara, and then I head for Charlie's, the world's greatest sports bar. Laurie's teaching her criminology class at William Paterson College tonight, so she won't be home until almost nine o'clock. Vince Sanders, the world's most disagreeable sports bar patron, is already at our regular table. In fact, based on the frequency that he's here, it's possible he's nailed to the chair.

The third member of our regular trio, Pete Stanton, is not here. This is not that unusual. Pete's a Paterson police lieutenant, and his job sometimes has erratic hours. Criminals don't punch a clock, so they can't be counted on to work nine to five.

"Hey, Vince. Pete's not here?"

"What tipped you off, bozo?"

"Happy again, are we?" I ask.

"Nets are down ten," he says. Vince bets the Nets, every game, no exceptions. It has not, over the years, been a profitable hobby.

"Who are they playing?" I ask.

"What's the difference? They couldn't beat the Campfire Girls JV team."

"Where's Pete?" I'm already a little depressed that Laurie is leaving tomorrow for Wisconsin. If I have to be alone with Vince for any length of time I might jump off a building.

"He's questioning your friend . . . the accountant guy."

"Sam?"

"Yeah."

"Why's he questioning him?"

"How the hell should I know?"

51

Going by my no-coincidences theory, if Sam is being questioned by the police after having talked to a friend who needed a criminal attorney, and after that friend died a violent death, the various elements have to be related.

I'm not sure what they would want to know from Sam, unless it's to discover what Barry Price told him. I'm also not sure why Pete, a Paterson cop, would be doing the questioning, though perhaps the cops assigned to the case wanted him along because he has jurisdiction.

I'm a little worried about Sam. I know he hasn't done anything wrong, but I don't want him to get caught up in something that could become a major hassle.

I'll call him and offer to help.

Just not tonight.

The border between the United States and Canada is more than five thousand miles long. It is the longest border in the world between two countries. It is also essentially undefended, except by civilian police forces. Customs and immigration offices are set up, and passports are required for entry into each country, but there is comparatively little security. While there is enormous focus on the border with Mexico, the one with Canada receives relatively scant attention.

Three hundred and ten miles of that border run along the state of North Dakota. It is a sparsely inhabited area, yet the terrain is not unfriendly. It is said that the entire Russian army could sneak into North Dakota, so long as they moved quickly and didn't play loud music.

The town of Bottineau has a little over two thousand people and is ten miles from the border. It has a small college and a winter park, and is best known for "Tommy," the world's largest turtle. Tommy is made from fiberglass, so feeding him is not a hardship for the citizens of Bottineau.

There is an airfield near the town, and that's where Carter arrived on a Dornier 328 jet. The superintendent in charge of the airfield took little notice of the plane, even though it was considerably larger and more expensive than most that landed there. It was capable of carrying thirty-four passengers, yet the only people on it were Carter and the pilot.

Carter rented a car and checked into a local hotel, in both cases using fake identification. When asked by the friendly hotel desk clerk why he was in town, he said it was to attend a meeting at Dakota College. That was of course false, but Carter wasn't particularly worried that the lie would in any way come back to haunt him. He wouldn't be there long enough.

Twelve hours before Carter's arrival, a contingent of thirty-two men had crossed the border, twelve miles north and three miles east of Bottineau. They were on foot but with ample supplies to sustain them on the trek that was ahead of them. These were men who had trained on a lot tougher terrain than this.

So Carter stayed out of sight, in the hotel, waiting for the call, which came thirty-six hours later, at shortly after 8:00 P.M. The men were just outside the airfield and were confident their presence had not been detected.

Carter drove out to the airfield at one o'clock in the morning. He wiped the car clean of fingerprints, an unnecessary precaution since he had worn gloves the entire time. Then he met the pilot and the thirty-two new arrivals out on the tarmac. The airport had long since closed; they were alone.

The plane took off in darkness, just before one thirty. The airport superintendent would report the strange circumstances to the FAA the next day, but little attention would be paid to it. No flight plan had been filed, so there was really nothing to follow up on anyway.

The residents of Bottineau, North Dakota, would never have any way of knowing that their town was the entry point for an invasion of the United States.

Sam figured he was the poorest person in the room. And it was a big room.

He had read in the newspaper that a memorial service was being held for Barry Price at a church in Kinnelon. It was by invitation only, but he thought he'd go anyway and maybe get a chance to pay his respects to Denise. He had felt guilty about leaving the other night, but he had considered himself an intruder.

He arrived early and was in fact not allowed admittance. However, he was in the parking lot when the limousine carrying Denise and some family members arrived. When she got out she saw him, thanked him for coming, and invited him inside.

It was an impressive turnout of at least three hundred people. Based on the cars in the parking lot, Sam estimated that two hundred ninety-nine of them were wealthy, with him being the only peasant in the group.

He had no idea if they were business associates of Barry, though he suspected that many were. They all sat solemnly as seven speakers extolled Barry's virtues, his philanthropy, and his tireless giving of money, time, and energy to friends, family, and community.

The only thing missing from the memorial service, Sam figured, was the deceased. Barry's body had still not been released by the coroner, so Sam assumed there would be a funeral ceremony at a future date. He had no idea why Denise wanted to go ahead with this now; maybe it was to achieve some kind of closure.

He also wondered if the police were bothering her. They had questioned him, Pete Stanton and the cop in the suit who had told Denise that Barry was dead. He identified himself this time as Lieutenant Jennings and did most of the talking, just wanting to know why Sam had been at the Price house that night and how he knew Denise and Barry. The whole thing seemed a little strange, and Sam hoped they'd at least wait awhile before intruding on Denise's grief.

Near the end of the ceremony, a woman

walked from the front of the room to the back, where Sam was sitting. She leaned over and said, "Some people are coming back to the house afterward. Mrs. Price would very much appreciate if you would do so as well."

"Of course."

George Costanza, eat your heart out. The Seinfeld character would often relish the prospect of such things as "make-up sex" after a fight with his girlfriend, or "conjugal-visit sex" when he was dating a lovely convicted embezzler.

Laurie and I pretty much never fight, and she won't be going to prison any time soon, so those two specialty sex options are not available to me. But that's okay, because tonight I'm going to have "going-away sex."

We're going to dinner first, which is fine, because I'm hoping that I'm going to need my strength. We are eating at the Bonfire, which has been my favorite Paterson restaurant for as long as I can remember.

It's a really nice dinner, except for the parts where Laurie keeps reminding me about her trip tomorrow. She doesn't do it to annoy me, but mentioning things like what she needs to pack or what time she wants to get to the airport are unwelcome reminders that she's leaving.

I tell her about Pete's questioning of Sam, and she agrees with me that it's likely that the out-of-town cops needed Pete because of his local jurisdiction. She also does not see it as ominous, but rather just a case of the police covering all bases. It's a high-profile death in a plane crash, the kind of case where the authorities would want to make sure they are invulnerable to future second-guessing or criticism.

We're home by nine o'clock, which means I'd like to be in bed by about nine oh three. Laurie has a different idea; she wants us to have a glass of wine and listen to music. Unfortunately, in situations like this it's usually Laurie's ideas that carry the day.

She leaves it to me to pick the music. This is not as easy as it sounds. I want it to be something that she likes and that will put her in the mood for sex. But I don't want her to like it too much, because then she might want to listen longer.

It can't be too lively, because that could take her out of that mood. But it can't be too mellow, because it could make her doze off. Sleep, in a situation like this, is the mortal enemy.

I choose an Eagles CD, but only time will

tell if it's going to work. We sit on the couch with Tara lying on the floor at our feet, talking occasionally but mostly sipping and listening. It is extraordinarily nice, not so much so that I don't wish we could cut it short, but nice nonetheless.

Finally, after an hour that seems like a very pleasant week, Laurie takes my hand and says, "Let's go upstairs."

"If you insist," I say.

She smiles. "You think you're going to get lucky?"

"There's no luck involved, babe."

We walk up the steps, Tara trailing behind us. She's seen this movie before, and I can't tell whether she approves or not. But I'm certainly not going to worry about it.

Laurie's in bed and I'm about to join her when the phone rings. "You want to get that?" she asks.

"Not even if I knew it was the lottery commission calling to congratulate me," I say. "The machine can get it."

The machine does get it, and the screened voice is Sam's. "Andy, it's me, Sam. Please pick up."

He sounds worried and upset, and Laurie and I make eye contact. Since her eyes are telling me to pick up the phone, I break off

61

contact. Whatever it is can wait until tomorrow.

"Andy, come on, you've got to be home. This is important . . . I need your help."

Now I've got no choice. I want to be there for Sam, but I want to be there later. The problem is, Laurie watching me ignore a friend in trouble would likely be a major turnoff.

What to do . . . what to do?

I pick up the phone. "Sam, are you hanging off the edge of a cliff by your fingernails?"

"No, I . . ."

I'm hoping that the big crisis is that Crash has kennel cough. "Then call me tomorrow."

"Andy, please . . . I need your help."

It was surreal. Everybody had left at least an hour before, and Sam and Denise were in her den, talking and reflecting on the Barry they knew. A couple of times Sam made comments about leaving, but Denise obviously did not want him to go yet. It was as if his walking out the door would put the final end to Barry, and she would have to face the pain alone.

It was almost nine o'clock when the knock on the door came. To Sam it was eerily like the other night, when Jennings and the other cop came to tell Denise about the crash.

Obviously Denise had the same sensation, because she commented that she had not buzzed anyone in through the main gate, and with a slight, sardonic laugh on the way to the door, said, "I hope this works out better than last time."

It didn't.

Once again Jennings was leading the way, but this time he had three other officers with him, and they weren't looking sympathetic. It all happened in a blur, but within seconds Denise was in handcuffs and Jennings was reading her her Miranda rights.

This time Sam heard every word he said, including, "You are being charged with the murder of Barry Price."

All Denise could say was, "No, no . . . this can't be happening." She looked back at Sam as she was being led out the door, silently imploring him to help her, but that was simply not within his power.

Jennings lingered behind to talk to Sam. "You seem to spend a lot of time here," he said.

"She's my friend," Sam said.

Jennings nodded. "No doubt about that. See you soon."

Once Jennings left, Sam saw everyone get into their two cars and drive off. He realized he should have asked where they were going, so he ran to his own car to follow them.

They didn't drive particularly quickly; there was certainly no need for sirens. They already had what they were going after.

It wasn't long before Sam's fear and concern turned to anger at how Denise was being treated and about Jennings's veiled comments about Sam's possible involvement.

It made no sense. Denise and Sam were nowhere near the plane or the airport when it crashed. In fact, Jennings himself could provide the alibi for them: he saw them in the house soon after the event.

What could they possibly be claiming? That Denise somehow sabotaged the plane so it would fall to the earth? Did they really think she had that expertise? It was ridiculous on its face. Jennings had to know that, so why the hell was Denise on the way to jail?

Sam decided that he had to call Andy. He couldn't imagine that Denise had access to a top criminal attorney, especially since Barry had inquired about Andy in the first place. If Barry didn't know one, then Denise certainly wouldn't. Any lawyers Barry had occasion to use would be more corporate, financial types.

Sam knew Andy had said he didn't want another client, and he respected that, but he thought he could convince him to at least get Denise through this initial process.

So he made the call.

And he begged.

The Morristown County people are well versed on modern jail techniques. Their leading technique is to make it as difficult as possible for defense attorneys, obviously including defense attorneys who no longer want to be defense attorneys.

I've brought Laurie with me, although this is not the way I had planned for us to spend this time. I'm actually surprised she was willing to come, but she didn't resist when I made the suggestion.

Sam is sitting in the lobby when we arrive, and he just about jumps out of his chair when he sees us. "Thanks for coming, guys. I had nowhere else to turn."

"Why don't you tell us everything you know?" He hadn't done so over the phone. I figured we might as well wait so that he could tell us in person.

It turns out he doesn't know much and is basically able only to describe the arrest as it took place.

"So no details about how she might have done it?" I ask.

"She didn't do it."

"I'm talking about their theory of the case."

"Right. No . . . no details at all. Andy, it is simply not possible that she could have murdered Barry."

Sam has seen this woman only a couple of times since high school, so I'm not quite prepared to accept his judgment as definitive, but I'm also not about to tell him that.

"They've made a mistake. She was with me when Barry died, but they won't listen to me. They'll listen to you."

At this point I don't know Denise Price, and she might well be a murderer. Certainly the police must have some evidence that she is, though they obviously still need to prove their case. But I'm not worried about her; I'm worried about Sam. His ex-girlfriend may have murdered her husband while he was there with her. It's not a huge leap for the cops to think that maybe a triangle was involved, with Sam in the role of Mr. Isosceles.

I leave Laurie with Sam and head for the desk, where the annoying ritual can begin. I identify myself as Denise Price's attorney, a stretch at the moment, and a temporary one at that. The knee-jerk reaction by the sergeant on duty is to tell me that she is undergoing the induction process, which, as I surely know, is time-consuming.

"She was brought in almost two hours ago," I exaggerate. "People have been inducted into Harvard fraternities faster."

"We have a process," he says.

"So do I. If I'm denied the ability to see my client in a reasonable time frame, I'll make the denier testify as to why. You feel like spending a day in court?"

"And leave all this?" he smiled, not exactly cowed by my threat.

Sam, anxious to know what is going on, comes up behind me. "Can I see her when you do?"

"What is this, camp visiting day?" the sergeant asks. "Go sit down over there."

It's another half hour before I'm ushered in to see Denise. She looks like every person I've ever seen in the midst of his or her first jail experience: scared and beaten down.

"Who are you?" she asks me.

"Andy Carpenter. I'm a defense attorney and a friend of Sam's."

"Barry mentioned you," she says, remembering. "I heard him ask Sam about you."

I've got a hunch that the key question in

the case is going to be why Barry asked Sam about me and whether he was involved in criminal activities. But it's way too premature for that.

"Do you have a lawyer, Denise?"

"For something like this? No. But you're going to help me, aren't you?"

"I am now, yes. Later on we can sort out what's best for you. For now the most important thing is that you talk to no one in here, about anything. If the police or prison authorities try to talk with you, just tell them to talk to me."

"Can you get me out of here? I have money."

"We will try to do that when you're brought into court, but it will be difficult, if not impossible."

"Why?"

"Because it is a murder case."

She looks bewildered. "His plane crashed. Barry's plane crashed. How could I have murdered him?"

"We'll find out why they think so; they have to tell us. But it won't be tonight, Denise. There is a process, and we have no choice but to go through it."

She nods her understanding, but she doesn't really get it, not yet. It's going to take a while to set in; it always does.

I continue. "I'll find out what I can, and I'll be back to see you tomorrow. What are you not going to do until then?"

"Talk to anyone."

"Good. I'll see you soon."

The look of pain on her face is intense. "What has happened to my life?" she asks.

It's one of a whole bunch of questions that I don't yet have the answer for.

I go back to the lobby area and tell Sam the little that transpired. He is frustrated that there's nothing to be done right now, but he understands it.

"Thanks, Andy," he says. "You'll stay on this?"

"For now. That's all I can promise. But either way she'll be well represented."

"She needs you," he says.

"Let's talk tomorrow, Sam. Go home."

"If I stay, you think there's any chance they'll let me see her?"

"Go home."

On the way back, Laurie asks what I thought of Denise Price.

"I didn't think she could be a murderer," I say, "but she could definitely be a murderer."

Among the many great things about Laurie is that when I say stuff like that, she understands exactly what I mean. The way to find out if someone is guilty is to get the facts and assess them, not make snap judgments based on personality and intuition.

"Sam seems somewhat taken with her," Laurie says, understating things considerably.

"I know. But if one is going to rekindle a relationship, there are probably better women to do it with than one facing trial for murdering her husband."

"So do you want to represent her?" she asks.

"Nope."

"What are you going to do?"

"I guess for now just get her through the arraignment, assess the situation, accumulate the facts."

As I say "accumulate the facts," I steal a quick glance at Laurie, which is a major mistake, and she catches me on it.

"So that's why you wanted me with you here tonight."

Uh-oh. She knows that I want her to investigate the case, which would in turn prevent her from going back to Wisconsin. The only way out of this is probably for me to tell the truth, but since that's not really my style, I decide to lie some more.

"I don't know what you mean. I wanted you with me because I always want you with me. I love and adore you."

"That's bullshit," she says.

"Which part?"

"The part where you didn't admit you wanted me to get interested in the case so I would stay home and investigate it."

I snap my fingers. "Hey, that's an idea I didn't think of."

"Okay, here are my terms. I agree to *delay* my trip to help you investigate the situation —"

I jump in. "Deal."

"I'm not finished," she says. "You agree to

work the case full-time until we get an answer."

"Deal."

She continues. "And you take on Denise Price as a client if we think she may be wrongly accused."

I'm stuck here; I can't ask her to take on an assignment if I'm not willing to do the same. "If we strongly feel that's the case, then it's a deal," I say grudgingly.

"I'm still not finished," she says. "Because I'm not leaving, you agree to give up your chance at going-away sex tonight."

I think we may have hit on a deal breaker. "What about if we do the whole wine and music thing again? Just maybe a shorter version?"

We're quiet for a while, and I'm trying to figure out if she's really going to put off her trip. I don't want to blow it, but the curiosity is killing me.

"So you're not leaving tomorrow?" I ask.

"No."

I shouldn't, but I ask, "Why?"

"I guess because investigating is what I do, and I'm looking forward to getting back into it. But I also like to watch you, to see you engaged."

"You mean the other kind of engaged?

Not the we're-going-to-get-married engaged?"

She smiles. "Yes, the other kind."

"Because either kind is fine," I say. "You know that."

Another smile. "Yes, I know that."

Then she looks over at me and says, "Andy, you don't ever have to worry about me leaving you."

"You did once." I say it in a light tone, but it's a subject that I will never regard as anything other than deadly serious.

"I know that, but I came back. And I'll never leave again."

"Anything is possible," I say.

"Then it's possible you'll leave me?"

I think for a moment. "Anything is possible. Except for that."

The manhunt lasted for only nine hours and ended in disaster. Undercover cop Drew Keller's car had remained in the parking lot behind the Concord, New Hampshire, bar, but Keller was gone. Patrons said he left with the man identified as Rodney Larsen, which fit with what Drew had recorded in several reports about his investigation. But the fact that his car was there and he had not called in was a thoroughly ominous sign. Drew would never have voluntarily gone off with Rodney without any possibility of backup.

With one of their own in obvious danger, every officer was called in to join in the search. Unfortunately, all that would have been required was one officer, manning the 911 line.

A call came in from a service station owner four miles from the bar. He opened in the morning, went into the back room, and discovered the horrific carnage.

Detective Lieutenant Clarence Burke took charge of the investigation and analyzed the crime scene. There were four dead bodies including Drew, all shot. Drew and Rodney were each killed with one bullet to the head, while the other two men were shot twice each.

Burke immediately distrusted what he was looking at. It was set up as if a firefight had taken place, but to Burke's trained eye, the pieces didn't fit, or at least there was one key piece missing. And that key piece had to be a fifth person, who had fled the scene.

Drew had been shot in the center of the forehead, so there was no question that he had died instantly. Therefore, by definition he had to have shot the others before he was hit himself.

But if Drew had shot the others before taking a bullet himself, it would mean that one of the other men, already mortally wounded, had nonetheless fired off a shot with perfect accuracy, killing Drew. It was certainly possible, but very, very unlikely.

There were also no stray bullet holes around the room; it seemed that every shot had hit its target. In a chaotic situation like this would have to have been, that simply was not credible.

There had to have been a fifth person in the room. Since Drew would obviously have been his prime target, he would have likely shot Drew first. What didn't make sense is why he would then have killed his three colleagues, if that's what they were.

It seemed to Burke highly unlikely that Drew had even fired a shot. If he had gone to the service station involuntarily, as was almost certainly the case, they would have taken his gun.

Ballistics would determine a lot of what happened, and Burke had the feeling that Drew's gun would be found to have fired the rounds that killed the other three men. But even though a gun was in the fallen Drew's hand, Burke would bet his pension that Drew had never actually pulled the trigger. He would never have been let into that room with his gun, Burke knew. It must have been thrust into his hand after he was dead.

So the investigation would begin, and Burke would not rest until he found the missing man, a mass murderer and cop killer. And not that he needed extra motivation, but Burke had some. Drew Keller had been his friend.

Burke had an additional obligation. Drew was investigating people who had spoken about killing "a big shot." Their threat hadn't been independently determined to be real, but the fact that there were now four dead bodies made it instantly credible.

Concord being the state capital, there had to be some concern that the big shot who was targeted was a political figure, perhaps even the governor. And if Burke was right about the way the killings went down, then the operation might still be intact.

Anyone who could kill four people could make it five. Or more.

So Burke went to his captain with the request that the FBI be alerted. If there was any suspicion of an assassination plot, that was protocol, and the captain instantly agreed.

The FBI was called in, and security around the governor and other state officials was immediately increased.

What they didn't realize was that the effort was wasted, that Concord had just become one of the few places where no one was in danger.

Laurie and I head back to the jail at 9:00 A.M. On the way, she calls the friend in Wisconsin who was going to pick her up at the airport, to tell her that she's not coming. She asks the friend to tell all her other friends the news.

I feel guilty about it, but I'll get over it. Laurie exercised free will in deciding to stay home; I didn't and couldn't coerce her, much as I would have wanted to. She loves investigative work and has missed it, so this gives her a chance to be happy. And, naturally, her not going makes me happy.

Of course, not everyone is happy. Not Barry Price, whose murder basically enabled all this happiness. And not Denise Price, who is stuck in jail for a murder she may or may not have committed.

Happiness is a zero-sum game.

We've run into quite a bit of traffic, thanks to a broken light up ahead that is just flashing red. It's bumper-to-bumper, and a car trying to enter from a strip mall on our right side has pretty much no chance to get in.

The male driver of that car looks at me, and I wave for him to enter in front of us. He does so, without waving back.

"Uh-oh," says Laurie, knowing what's coming.

"Did you see that?" I ask. "The guy didn't even wave." To me, not waving thanks in a situation like that is deserving of imprisonment.

"Shocking," Laurie says.

"Now we have to sit behind that guy in this traffic? He's going to get where he's going before we do?"

"How do you know where he's going?"

"You're missing the point," I say.

"So you don't let them in to help them out. You do it to look like a really nice guy and get thanked?"

"Of course. Why would I care if that guy was stuck in that strip mall? I wish I had a BB gun with me. I'd shoot out one of his tires."

Laurie shakes her head sadly. "Mentally speaking, you need a lot of help."

"Maybe so, but I'll tell you this: if I got that help, I'd wave to the people who helped me."

I call Hike Lynch, who functions as my cocounsel on the rare occasions that we have a case. The fact that I work with Hike is reason enough never to take on another client. He's a complete pessimist, with an uncanny ability to always see the negative side of any situation.

Hike now has a girlfriend, which in itself defies all logic. She noticed he was depressed, which doesn't exactly make her Freud, and convinced him to get a battery of tests to determine whether he should be on medication. He was ultimately judged not to be clinically depressed, an outcome that further depressed him.

When starting a conversation with most people, I would automatically ask, "How are you?" or "How's it going?" I have learned not to do that with Hike, because I'm guaranteed to be bombarded with a litany of awful things that have happened to him in the last twenty-four hours, often including defective and disgusting bodily functions.

So instead I say, "Hey, I never got your e-mail." I had asked him to find out the name of the prosecutor in Morris County who is handling Denise Price's case and set up a meeting for me.

"I can't type," he says. "I tore a cuticle."

"Oh."

"Then I pulled on it and it kept coming. I ripped it off almost to my elbow."

"I didn't know cuticles go as far as the elbow," I say as Laurie stares at me in amazement.

"Mine does," he says. "Or at least it used to, before I ripped it off."

"Hold on, Hike. Let me put Laurie on; you can read the information to her."

I hand the phone to Laurie, one of the meaner things I've done in the past decade, and she frowns but gets the information from Hike. It takes a while, and to get off the phone she finally has to lie and tell Hike we've arrived at the prison. To get off the phone with Hike, I would check into prison.

There are two types of photographs that one should never rely on to judge how good-looking a person is. One is the pictures of themselves that people put on dating Web sites. The other, even less reliable, is a mug shot.

The dating photos are designed to make the person look better and therefore date-able. Of course, unless the hope is to have a relationship that never gets beyond phone sex, eventually the truth will be revealed.

The mug shots always, and I mean *always*, make people look worse than they normally do. That's why you will never find people using their mug shot on a dating site. Of course, if they did, there might be other reasons not to date them besides their being bald or chubby or just weird looking.

I haven't seen the mug shot they took of Denise last night, but I'm sure it captured the way she looks when she's brought in to see us this morning: depressed, frightened, worried, miserable. It is the way every person looks when he or she is first imprisoned, because it is the way every person feels.

The other thing that the first exposure to prison life does is activate the denial mechanism in the brain. For example, Denise has no recollection that I told her bail in this case would be virtually impossible, and she is stunned when I repeat it.

"The reason you are in here is that the prosecutor believes he has convincing evidence that you are responsible for your husband's death. The only way you're going to get out of here is to convince a judge, or maybe a jury, that the prosecutor is wrong."

"How do we do that?" she asks.

"One of two ways. Demonstrate either that you didn't do it or that someone else did."

The pained expression doesn't leave her

face, which probably means she realizes neither of my described routes out of here is going to be quick or easy.

"Let's start with some questions," I say. "You said that you heard Barry ask Sam about me."

She nods. "Yes, but I overheard him. He didn't know I was listening."

"Why was Barry interested in a criminal defense attorney?"

"I didn't know that he was. I assumed you were a divorce lawyer."

"Barry was looking for a divorce?"

"It would not have surprised me. We weren't getting along for a while."

"What was the problem?"

"He didn't love me anymore," she says, starting to tear up. "He hadn't loved me for a while."

Laurie asks her first question. "Was there a third party involved?"

Denise nods. She seems on the edge of losing it but takes a moment to pull herself together. "There was no shortage of parties involved. But I doubt very much that Barry loved any of them either."

My keen ear notices that when Denise mentions Barry, she doesn't throw in the obligatory "May he rest in peace." This was a woman scorned, not necessarily a good thing to be if you're going on trial for the murder of the scorner.

I sneak a glance at Laurie, who is probably focusing on the positive in all this. If there are other women, women whom Barry had obviously not left his wife for, then they are all potential suspects.

"So you have no idea why Barry might have needed a criminal attorney?"

She shakes her head. "No. Probably something involving his business. He seemed especially preoccupied the last few weeks. It's one of the reasons I thought he was getting ready to leave me."

"Do you know much about Barry's business?" Laurie asks.

"No, he kept me as far away from it as possible."

"Who would be the best person for us to talk to about it?"

"Mark Clemens," she says without hesitation. "He's the number-two person in the firm. Sort of Barry's protégé."

"Have you spoken to him since Barry died?"

"Yes. He told me we'll need to talk about the business when I'm ready. I guess I own most of it now."

We question Denise some more for anything she might know about Barry that would make him a target for murder, but there's nothing there, or nothing she's prepared to reveal.

"Do you know anything about the mechanical workings of airplanes?" I ask.

"Nothing at all; I can barely operate a light switch. Anyone who knows me realizes that."

I explain to Denise that she is going to be brought to an arraignment, which is the next time I will see her. I repeat that she is not to talk to anyone about anything without me being present, and she seems to understand that.

"I haven't said a word," she says, "not even to the person . . ." She stops in mid-sentence.

"What's the matter?" Laurie asks.

Denise smiles slightly. "I just realized I have a cell mate. I guess I expected to go through my entire life without a cell mate."

It's the first evidence I've seen that Denise has a sense of humor.

She's going to need it.

I know nothing about the prosecutors in Morris County. I generally try cases against the Passaic County prosecutors, and my unfamiliarity with their Morris counterparts leaves me at a disadvantage. I've learned the idiosyncrasies and habits of the Passaic group, and I'm able to effectively use that knowledge. I won't be able to do that here.

On the other hand, the Morris lawyers and judges don't yet despise me, don't dream of the day when they conduct a murder trial in which the role of victim is played by Andy Carpenter. So this is sort of refreshing.

Hike has set up an appointment with Thomas Bader, the prosecutor handling the Denise Price case. The fact that Bader was willing to meet so quickly, without hassle, probably indicates that he's happy with his case and has little to hide. Or maybe he's just a friendly guy.

Bader is in his late thirties, maybe six two and a hundred and seventy pounds, with a face more than vaguely like Matt Damon's. I'm glad Laurie waited out in the lobby.

We exchange fake pleasantries and then I say, "My cocounsel said you were very cooperative in agreeing to see me on short notice. I appreciate that."

"That was your cocounsel?" he asks with obvious surprise. "The guy with the foot-long cuticle?"

"The very one," I say. "Goes clear up to the elbow, and then loops around. When can I expect discovery?"

"Starting right about now," he says agreeably. "We've only got a couple of boxes of it copied so far. I can send it to your office, or you can take it with you." This level of pleasant cooperation is another bad sign. He knows that I know this, so he grins and says, "We've got a strong case."

"You don't mind if I don't take your word for that, do you?" I ask.

"I expect the great Andy Carpenter to fight every step of the way."

I've never been called "the great Andy Carpenter" before. It has a nice ring to it. It would be really nice if Laurie could incorporate it into her everyday conversation. Like "Wow, I just slept with the great Andy

Carpenter" or "The great Andy Carpenter just took out the garbage."

I'd like to come up with questions that would get Bader to use the phrase again, but I can't think of any. So instead I go with, "Any surprises in there?"

"Well, the victim died of botulism."

I try my best to conceal a very significant level of surprise. "So your theory is he was dead before the plane hit the ground?"

"Not *my* theory," he says. "It's the coroner's conclusion, though he doesn't say exactly that. Price could have been paralyzed; botulism does that before it kills you. Anyway, it's preliminary, but he tells me that's where it's going to end up."

"And how do you tie this to Denise Price?"

He smiles tolerantly but stands up, indicating that the meeting has come to the end. "It's all in the discovery documents," he says. "You may not find it enjoyable reading."

"Let's let the 'great Andy Carpenter' be the judge of that," I say.

He laughs and extends his hand. "Happy to." Then, "You seem like a nice enough guy."

"That surprises you?"

He nods. "I spoke to some friends in the

Passaic County office. You're in no danger of them electing you Miss Congeniality at the Defense Attorney Ball."

"Damn . . . I just bought a dress."

I load the two boxes of discovery documents into the car, and Laurie and I head for home.

"He was poisoned," I say. "Botulism."

"Uh-oh." There's no hard-and-fast rule, but poison is more often the weapon of choice for women than for men.

"Could have been ingested accidentally," I say.

"Right. He was out on a nature walk, and he picked a piece of fruit off a botulism tree." As a former cop, Laurie is considerably more likely than I am to come down on the prosecution side. That can actually be helpful to me, in terms of my understanding how the other side is thinking.

"There're a lot of ways it could have happened, and a lot of people who could have caused it to happen."

"Or maybe Sam's high school sweetheart isn't quite so sweet."

"Poor Sam," I say.

"He'll get over it."

"But it will hurt. If this went down as the prosecution says, then she was going to kill

Sam as well. She expected him to be on the plane."

"Until that dog intervened."

I nod. "Good old Crash."

The garage was the tip-off. Detective Burke realized it even before Special Agent Ricardo Muñoz, the FBI agent he was guiding through the investigation. Not that Muñoz didn't notice the obvious; it just took him a split second longer.

So far the relationship between the two men was going uncharacteristically smoothly. Burke was investigating the death of a fellow cop, a friend, and he made it clear to Muñoz that he was not backing off. It was his case.

Muñoz was fine with that. Rather than adopt the more traditional FBI scornful attitude toward the locals, he recognized that since he was on assignment out of the New York City office and unfamiliar with Concord, Burke could be a help in showing him the lay of the land.

Their first stop was at the home of Alex and Rodney Larsen, the brothers whose bodies were found in the service station with Drew Keller's. It was a small house in a very run-down area, no surprise since records showed that both men, while listing their occupation as auto mechanics, were receiving unemployment insurance.

The front door was locked, so Burke tried the garage, which opened. And there it was, pristine clean and in mint condition, a new, fully loaded pickup truck.

"Unemployment must pay more than it used to," Burke said.

The rest of the house revealed similar nuggets. There was a new TV, an apparently new computer, and a DVD player that was still in the box.

Burke called in the license number on the truck and learned that it was not stolen but in fact purchased by Alex Larsen six days prior. Muñoz, in the meantime, was phoning in a request to get the financial and banking records of the two brothers as soon as possible.

Burke had arranged for a forensics team to meet them at the house, and the team showed up a few minutes after they had entered. They were to retrieve as many prints as they could. Someone had killed the brothers, and it could well have been a coconspirator. If so, at some point he might have been in this house.

Burke and Muñoz carefully searched the house but did not turn up any obvious evidence that they could use. They impounded an old computer that was on the desk, as well as the new one, which would be examined by experts.

As they were getting ready to leave, Muñoz got a phone call from his office. When he got off, he said to Burke, "Alex Larsen had one hundred thousand dollars wired into his account two weeks ago."

"From who?"

"They're running that down now. There is eight thousand in the account now; I've got a hunch he didn't put the rest into T-bills."

"So not only were they going to kill a big shot, they were being paid real money to do so," Burke said. "You think it was their employer who decided they were expendable?"

"Maybe your friend showing up scared him off," Muñoz said.

"Or maybe the employer looked at the way they were spending the money and the way they talked to Drew and decided they were too stupid to rely on or allow to live."

"You got a lot of big shots around here?" he asked, though he knew the answer.

Burke nodded. "It's the state capital;

we've got a few."

"I think the plan was to reduce the number."

Reading the discovery material presents a bad news/bad news situation. As Thomas Bader had said, these are only the beginning in what will be a series of discovery documents. But what is here is damaging enough to Denise Price.

Barry Price probably died of botulism poisoning; the injuries he suffered when thrown from the plane were all, according to the coroner, likely postmortem. It's hard to tell exactly, since the effects of the poison had certainly set in long before the crash. It's entirely possible that the impact mercifully finished the job.

I take a few minutes to Google botulism, and the facts can be molded to fit the prosecution's theory and time line, as I expected they would.

There were traces of the poison found in a basement sink drain in the Prices' house, which certainly tends to implicate Denise.

She and Barry are the two obvious candidates to have had access to that sink, and he could safely be characterized as being in the clear.

Another troublesome little tidbit is that Denise worked as a pharmacist's assistant for two years before meeting and marrying Barry. It just contributes to the notion that she would have been capable of preparing the poison.

There is no possibility of successfully arguing suicide in this case. It makes no sense that Barry would deliberately ingest a poison and then get on that plane. If he wanted to kill himself, he could have just taken the poison, or more likely just gotten on the plane and flown it into the ground. There is no logical reason to do both.

The obvious conclusion, though not mentioned in the documents, is that the killer gave Barry the poison before he was going to fly, in the hope that the crash and subsequent explosion would incinerate the body and remove the chemical residue.

This too points to Denise; she knew that Barry was making the flight.

The police had moved quickly, and there are already interviews with friends of the Prices who claim that their marriage was a troubled one. None of them are yet ready to believe that Denise could have done it, but that will not be a help to her attorney. Somebody did it, and there is no reason the jury would consider her incapable of being the one.

So that's the bad news.

And here's the other bad news: I'm finding myself getting into it.

I'm reading these pages as if I am Denise Price's attorney, and worse yet, I'm semi-okay with that. It's forcing me to think logically, to start to problem-solve, and rather than dreading the work, I'm sort of looking forward to it.

Is industriousness contagious? Can you catch a work ethic from someone? And is there a cure?

"This is your fault," I say to Laurie, who is reading the pages as well.

"What did I do now?"

"You made me get involved with this, and it is stirring my long dormant freeze-dried work juices."

"You're leaning toward taking the case?" she asks, obviously surprised.

"Unless I wake up tomorrow having come to my senses."

"Are you reading something that makes you think Denise Price is innocent?"

"Nope."

"Don't misunderstand me, Andy. I think your getting back to work is great, but I thought your standard was you needed to believe in your client."

"It is. But these pages, this investigation, are the work of the prosecution. And I'm more interested in what I'm not reading."

"What might that be?"

"I'm not reading that Barry Price was looking for a criminal attorney."

"So what if he was?"

"Well, unless he was worried about being charged with felony masturbation, his crime had to involve other people. People he either stole from or stole with or whatever. People who might have had a reason to kill him. The fact that he was killed the day he was looking for a criminal attorney creates a reasonable doubt, at least in my mind."

She points to the documents. "This evidence is pretty compelling, and there might be more to follow."

"It's their job to assign guilt. My job is to develop my own facts and to attack their case."

She smiles. "You have a job?"

"I'm afraid I might. Botulism is as bad as it gets as a way to die. I'd have to be convinced that the Denise Price I met, who Sam swears by, could do that to someone she lived with for twenty years."

"You don't know what went on behind their closed doors."

"How would you kill me?" I asked.

"That's easy. I'd get you to commit suicide."

"How?"

"Make you talk about relationships, bring you to couples therapy, buy you a treadmill, disconnect your cable TV, get you a subscription to the ballet . . ."

"What an awful way to go," I say.

She smiles. "Just don't get on my bad side."

"As far as I can tell — and believe me, I have looked from all angles — you don't have a bad side."

I'm human; I make mistakes on a case, and this first one is a beauty. I'm driving up to Connecticut to check out the scene where Barry Price's plane went down. It's not likely I'll learn anything, but that's not my mistake.

My mistake is bringing Hike along.

It's about a two-hour-and-forty-five-minute ride, which means that round-trip will be five and a half hours, alone in a car with Hike. My only way out, and it is one I am seriously considering, is driving off the George Washington Bridge on the way.

Hike is going to be working with me on the case, if I make the final decision to take it, so I want him to start focusing on it. I always begin by going to the scene of the crime, usually with Laurie, since she is my lead investigator.

But because this was a plane crash, the benefit of going is not likely to be significant.

Therefore I think Laurie is better off working on things in Jersey, hence my invitation to Hike.

He spends the first half hour of the ride reading discovery documents, so it's mercifully quiet. Then all of a sudden he says, "Wow . . . botulism. That's pretty cool."

"You're a botulism fan?"

"I know a lot about poisons; it's sort of a hobby. Botulism isn't my favorite, but it's in the top twenty."

I'm not sure I want to go down this path, so I don't say anything. It doesn't dissuade Hike from continuing the discussion.

"Did you know there are at least four thousand undiscovered poisons? And don't get me started on viruses."

I have absolutely no intention of getting him started on viruses. "How do you know about them if they're not discovered?"

"Statistics. We know how many they find each year, so you just extrapolate it out. It's basic math." He looks at me with obvious surprise. "You don't read the CDC reports on human toxins?"

"No, but I get *Entertainment Weekly.*" Please God, let this conversation be over.

It isn't. "You want to know my favorite poison?" Hike asks.

"Not even a little bit."

"It's sarin. First it collapses your lungs; you feel like there's a hippo sitting on your chest. Then you start unloading, I mean stuff starts coming out of every opening you've got, and some you didn't know you had —"

"Hike, that's —"

"Of course, it's all over in like fifteen minutes," he says with apparent sadness.

"You want it to last longer?"

"Depends on who takes it."

Right about now I'd be inclined to take some, but I don't mention this to Hike, because he probably has a pocket full of it. Instead I just point to the documents he hasn't gone through yet. "Keep reading," I say.

We're met at the scene by Terry Bresnick, a retired investigator for the National Transportation Safety Board. As is the case in all plane crashes, NTSB is conducting the investigation, and the scene is still under their control.

Thomas Bader, in the homestretch in his campaign to be named "most cooperative prosecutor in America," has arranged for us to get access.

I met Terry on a case about ten years ago. He was a witness for the prosecution, and I cross-examined him. I scored a lot of points, but he knew his stuff, and I thought he held his own pretty well.

But he was angry about the way I treated him, and once the trial was over, he came to my office to tell me so. Since he's about six five and two hundred and forty pounds, I was less than delighted to see him. I would have hidden behind Edna, had she been in that day.

Within three minutes, we left my office, went over to Charlie's, and had some beer and burgers, and we have been friends ever since. I've done him a couple of favors with legal work in recent years, and he's always talked about wanting to repay me in kind. That's why he jumped at this opportunity when I called.

Terry has gotten the lay of the land in advance of our arrival, helped along by his old friends from the agency. Because of that, he is able to take Hike and me on a quick tour. There is a large area that has been fenced off by the NTSB, and Terry walks us to the back end of the area, which is wooded.

"The plane hit in those trees," he said, "and it started to break up. That's where the pilot was thrown."

"Is it possible to tell where he was in the plane when it happened?"

"That's easy. He was still belted into the pilot seat." He points toward an open, grassy area. "He came down over there. I'm told the body was pretty well intact."

"Where did the rest of the plane come down?" Hike asks.

"I'll show you." He walks us what seems to be at least a quarter mile away, and we can see the wreckage strewn over a large area.

"Any chance the plane exploded?"

"You mean in flight, as if the explosion was the cause?"

"Yes."

"Certainly doesn't seem like it, not based on the way the wreckage lays out. But I don't have access to all the facts."

"So why did it come down?" I ask.

He hesitates. "I'll tell you what I've heard, okay? But you didn't hear it from me."

I nod. "Deal."

"It's early, but they've found nothing mechanically wrong with the plane, and it was serviced and inspected the morning of the flight. There was some rain, but not enough to have caused a problem, and minimal wind."

"So pilot error?"

He shrugs. "If by 'error' you mean he didn't do anything. There's no sign he took any action at all, and certainly he never got on the radio to say anything. Maybe the black boxes will reveal more, but I doubt it. I wouldn't be surprised if he had a heart attack or passed out for some reason."

Obviously Terry hasn't been told about the poison, and there's no reason for me to mention it. He's confirmed the prosecution's theory that Barry Price was incapacitated, even if he doesn't know why.

Any defense that Denise Price couldn't have killed her husband because she didn't have a knowledge of airplane mechanics is off the table. At this point it's not a crowded table.

On the way back, Hike asks, "You gonna take the case?"

"I think so."

"What happened to the client-has-to-be-innocent thing?"

"We don't know that she did it."

"You mean because she hasn't confessed and there's no video of her administering the poison?"

I nod. "There is that." Then, "Are you in?" I'm asking Hike if he wants to work on the case. It will mean a big commitment from him in time and energy, to say nothing of the fact that a trial like this can be emotionally wrenching, draining everything out of a lawyer in what can ultimately be a losing cause.

On the other hand, Hike would be getting paid, which for him is a surefire antidote for wrenching and draining.

"Sure," he says. "Regular rate?"

"Regular rate," I confirm.

He smiles. "Let's go get 'em."

"Nothing that happens today will be significant."

"Why?" Denise asks, obviously disappointed. We're in an anteroom in the courthouse, and I am prepping her for the arraignment, set to begin in a few minutes.

"It's all a formality. They will read the charges against you, and you should not show any expression at all when they do, just stare straight ahead. Then they'll ask how you plead, and you should simply say, 'Not guilty, Your Honor.' "

"Then what?"

"Then we prepare for trial."

Like most defendants, Denise is constantly expecting someone to snap his or her fingers and realize in the moment that she is not guilty and that this is all a mistake. I've been trying to make her understand that it won't happen, that it's going to be a difficult grind, but it always takes a while to internalize it. It is going to take waking up in a jail cell, day after boring day, to get the message across.

"Denise, a few of the witnesses the prosecution spoke to mentioned that they attended a party at your house the night before Barry died. Sam was there as well."

"Right. The parties were more Barry's idea, and we had them periodically."

"Who would attend?"

"There were a lot of his clients and some friends. Barry thought it was best to mix the two, that it would make the conversation more interesting to have people from different backgrounds."

"How many people were there that night?"

"Probably fifty or so."

"Can you write out a list of the people you remember being there?"

"I can try; I'm not sure if I can remember everybody."

"Did you argue with Barry that night?" I ask, knowing that there have been references to that in the witness reports, and Sam had mentioned it as well.

"I argued with Barry almost every night. We usually tried not to do it in public, but that time we did."

"Okay," I say. "Please work on that list."

I open the door and we enter the adjacent

courtroom. It probably seats about seventy-five people, and every seat is taken. The media have adopted this as a story worthy of covering, probably because of Barry's money and the fact that Denise is good-looking.

Denise recoils slightly when she sees all the people; this is humiliating for her. Of course, when the final resolution comes, she will either have vindication, or if not, then humiliation will be the least of her problems.

I recognize only a few people in the room. Hike is at the defense table, Thomas Bader is at the prosecution table with three assistant attorneys, and Sam is in the front row.

Judge Calvin Hurdle takes his place behind the bench. I've never tried a case before him, so I've asked around, and I've been told he's a no-nonsense judge.

Of course, that really doesn't help me much, because I haven't exactly run into a whole bunch of nonsense judges. You don't find too many judges who are real practical-joking cutups, putting shaving cream in lawyers' shoes and whoopee cushions on jurors' chairs.

Judges are a predictable group, disciplinarians who pride themselves on maintaining total control of their courtrooms. They have their humor genes surgically removed when they take the oath. It's one of the reasons they can't stand me.

Judge Hurdle goes through some housekeeping issues, and then the charges are read. Denise follows my instructions well and stares impassively throughout. My reason for cautioning her about this has nothing to do with the judge or any of the court members; I simply don't want the media characterizing her in a negative way. The people who matter are not here today. They are out there in the real world, and they will be reading and hearing about the case through the media. And after they do, some of them will make their way to the jury box.

Finally it comes time to enter her plea, and Denise does so in a clear, firm voice. A trial date is set, and Judge Hurdle taps his gavel and adjourns the session. A guard comes to escort Denise out, and she looks at me pleadingly, fear evident in her eyes.

I really want to help this woman, and I really, really hope she didn't administer a deadly poison to her husband.

I go out through the back to avoid waiting reporters. I'm not above playing them for my benefit; I'm just not in a position to do so now. At some point I will be, and then

I'll be Mr. Accessible.

Sam comes along with me, asking, "How did it go?"

"Same as always. A nonevent."

"I just thought there was a nuance that I might have missed."

"Nope, it was a nuance-free zone. You on the team this time?" Sam has been a valuable member of our investigative team on previous cases, mostly because of his genius on a computer. He can hack into pretty much anywhere, getting information we might otherwise never have access to.

Unfortunately, he extended his responsibilities to the noncyber world on our last case without my approval, and he almost got killed in the process. Marcus saved him, but it shook him up very badly, as it should have, and may have cured him of his desire to be involved in this stuff.

It didn't.

"I'm in all the way, Andy. Just tell me what to do."

"Come on back to the office; we're going to talk about it."

Sam had driven out to the court with Hike but for some reason doesn't want to go back with him. I can't imagine why.

So Sam rides with me, which means I have to spend forty-five minutes listening to what a great dog Crash is. This despite the fact that he's still recuperating and hasn't yet left the vet's office.

"He's amazing. I talk to him, and he understands what I'm saying."

"How do you know that?"

"I just know, I can tell. It's like we have this bond." He pauses a moment and then says momentously, "God sent this dog to me, Andy. He sent him to save my life, to prevent me from getting on that plane."

"Why didn't he just give you a flat tire?"

"Because this was a test, to see what I would do," Sam says.

"I hope he doesn't use the flat tire test on me. I don't even know how to work the jack."

We meet Hike, Laurie, and Marcus Clark at my office for the initial preliminary meeting we have on all cases. Everybody is by now used to having Marcus around, though it's impossible to totally get used to having Marcus around.

Marcus is the scariest, toughest individual on the planet, and he's particularly valuable if we need to do something that requires physical action, like, say, invading Argentina. I hope there's no violence involved in this case, but Marcus also has terrific investigative skills. As always, he'll work directly under Laurie, since she's the only one who's not scared to death of him.

Marcus almost never talks, and when he does he usually just utters barely comprehensible syllables. So it's left to everyone to ponder what he might be thinking, a hopeless task if ever there was one.

Edna is the last one to arrive, although mentally I think she is in tournament mode. When I ask her, "How is the preparation going?" she says, "Twenty-four."

"Twenty-four? What does that mean?" I ask.

"That's how many letters were in your question," she says. "Ability to count letters quickly is very helpful."

I nod. "Okay." And then I say, "Four," but she doesn't seem amused by my joke. All she does is sit at her desk, enveloped in thought, completely uninterested in our meeting or case. What's a four-letter word for unwillingness to work, first letter is *e*?

I start the meeting by bringing everyone up-to-date on the little that has happened so far and the information in the discovery documents that we have received.

"The prosecution's case is going to be mostly forensics," I say. "There will also be witnesses describing the state of the Prices' marriage, which they'll use to provide motive."

I'm distracted by Sam's phone, which is sitting on the desk. His screen saver is a series of pictures of Crash, which alternate automatically in a slide show. There are at least twenty pictures of him, all lying in the same dog run.

I continue. "I can tell you that while we will of course attack the prosecution's case, we're going to have to do much more. We're going to have to find the real killer, or at least point to a viable alternative."

I talk about the request by Barry Price to hire me as his attorney just before he died, and how that is an area we have to focus on.

"Where do we start?" Sam asks.

"We follow the money."

Mark Clemens thinks Denise is guilty. He won't come right out and say so, but that's certainly the impression I've been getting. He told me over the phone that he was really busy but he'd "clear the schedule" to see me, because "nothing is more important than finding out who did this."

The offices of the Price Group occupy an entire floor of a building on Thirty-fourth Street near Seventh Avenue in Manhattan. "Barry wanted to keep his commute as short as possible," Clemens explains, "which is why the office is near the Lincoln Tunnel and not Wall Street."

"Morristown to here is not exactly a short trip either," I point out.

Clemens smiles. "That's probably why Barry came in so rarely." Then, as if I might take that as criticism, he adds, "His home was fully stocked with electronics; it was the same as if he was in the office."

116

Clemens seems invested in my knowing what a legendary genius Barry was. His clients relied totally on his investment acumen, which seems to be why the firm has been so successful. Without Barry present, it's obvious Clemens is concerned that the clients might walk.

After ten minutes of listening to this praise, I feel like I'm stuck in goo. Since Clemens can't be more than thirty-five years old and Barry is the one who placed him in this no-doubt-lucrative job, his devotion is understandable. But it doesn't get me anywhere. Someone wasn't quite as enamored of Barry; in fact, that person killed him.

"So Barry made the investment decisions. What was your role?"

"Mostly new business. I brought in prospective clients, and Barry made the sale."

"How much money does the company invest?"

"Right now we have about eleven billion dollars in assets."

That's a lot of money; people have been murdered for less. "Any idea why Barry needed a criminal attorney?"

His tone immediately changes. "That's ridiculous. He was the most law-abiding person I've ever met. If I even hinted that we do something not criminal but just bending the rules slightly, he cut me off at the knees."

"He was looking for a criminal attorney the day he died."

"Are you trying to smear him? Is that what the defense is going to be?"

"I choose to think of it as finding the truth and defending my client," I say, but then decide to try another approach. "Why would he have been asking an outside accountant for help?"

Clemens's attitude has turned frosty. "I doubt that he was. But I would have no idea; certainly it would have to be something personal. The firm is well represented."

"Any idea who might want to kill him?"

"I believe the police have already made that decision," he says.

"And you think they're right?"

"It doesn't matter what I think, but I'll tell you what I know. I know that Barry's marriage was going to end, and I know that right now, at this moment, his wife is worth a hell of a lot of money. And I also know that Barry Price didn't have an enemy in the world."

The only way I've got a chance at helping Denise by asking this guy questions is if I do it on the witness stand.

"I'm going to need a list of your clients," I say.

"Why?"

"That's really not something I'm prepared to share with you."

"It's confidential."

"No it isn't," I say. "But if it makes it easier, I can subpoena it and then talk to each of your clients individually."

"I'll have to consult our attorneys about this."

"You do that. In the meantime, I'll get the subpoena ready. Maybe we can do a two-day deposition. It'll make us even closer."

Kyle Austin felt a little like he was a prisoner. It was a feeling he had some experience with, since he had spent one of his twenty-seven years in an actual prison.

The entire experience had been surreal, from the first time they had approached him, then actually receiving the first half of the money, and especially this trip they had arranged for him.

As he learned what it was they wanted him to do, it became obvious why they chose him. His army training, his lack of a job, his need for money, and his somewhat violent past all made him a perfect candidate. Kyle thought it was pretty funny that all those things that had seemed so negative for so long had suddenly combined to create this great opportunity.

At their request, he had driven from his hometown of Columbus, Ohio, to a rest stop off Route 80. There he was picked up by a guy in a small bus, sort of like what he imagined a party bus those rock stars use.

The guy didn't tell him his name, but he did explain the rules. The doors would be locked from the outside, and with the windows blackened, Kyle would not be able to see or go outside for the duration of the trip.

There was a wall between the driver's section and the main area of the bus, so that Kyle couldn't see out the front window, either. He could talk to the driver through an intercom, but it seemed unlikely that the guy might say anything that Kyle would be eager to hear.

There was enough to keep him comfortable. The bus came equipped with plenty of great food and drink, a television with DVD player, a bathroom, a comfortable bed, and even a shower if Kyle so desired.

It was clear to Kyle that the destination was to remain a secret, and when he asked how long a trip it would be, the driver said, "As long as it takes."

So they drove, twelve hours according to Kyle's watch, but that didn't tell him much, since he had no idea what direction they were traveling in or the speed the bus was going. They had taken his cell phone, probably because the GPS in it could have revealed his location.

The fact of the matter was that Kyle wasn't particularly worried; these guys had already paid him a hundred grand. They did that because he had value to them, and there was no reason to think that they would want to do anything to hurt their investment.

They finally arrived at their destination about 8:00 P.M., and Kyle was surprised by what he saw when he got off the bus. There were a series of buildings, almost like small barracks, set on what seemed like a small post or camp.

Kyle knew what army bases looked like; he had been an infantryman in Iraq, and this one seemed a little like a miniaturized version. He was led to one of the buildings and read the same ground rules as there had been on the bus. He'd be locked in the room with many creature comforts, but he was not to nose around.

Kyle noticed immediately that the food was ample and similar to that on the bus. The drinks, however, were another matter. There was no alcohol of any kind in the room, whereas on the bus he had put away a six-pack of beer.

They obviously wanted him clearheaded in the morning.

Kyle was awakened at six thirty by the guy who drove the bus and who was literally the only person he had seen since Ohio. He was friendly enough, but when Kyle asked if there were people in the other rooms, he just smiled and said, "Be ready in an hour."

Exactly one hour later, Kyle was ready, and the driver was back. He brought Kyle outside and they walked across a grassy area to the largest building. It was completely empty, except for some chalk markings on the floor.

The driver then brought him into an office off the main room, which also was empty, except for a large table and a man sitting in a chair.

The man was Carter, the only person in this entire operation whom Kyle had ever met before, the man who was in the process of making Kyle wealthy. He had a smile on his face as he watched Kyle stare at what was on the table.

It was a mock-up of a weapon, one Kyle was already very familiar with from his time in Iraq. They probably knew that; they seemed to know everything, so he figured it was why they came to him in the first place.

Kyle looked behind him and noticed that the driver had left the room, leaving only him and Carter.

"It's time for the training," Carter said.

"I already know how to use the real thing."

"You'll have a chance to demonstrate that, after you are trained according to our process."

Kyle wasn't about to argue; these people were paying the bills, and paying them well. "I've got plenty of time," he said.

Carter smiled and said, "Less than you think." He stood up. "Let's get started."

"Let's assume Barry Price wasn't holding up liquor stores," I say. "And he never murdered anyone or sold drugs."

I'm talking with Hike and Sam in my office, trying to figure out the best way to approach the investigation. "Let's further assume the reason he needed a criminal attorney had something to do with money, and very possibly the eleven billion dollars that he was responsible for."

"You think this was Madoff II?" Hike asks. "Maybe he was ripping off his clients or faking profits on their investments?"

"Those are certainly possibilities worth checking into. Or maybe insider trading or a hundred other things that I have no understanding of."

"That's more my area," Sam says.

I nod. "I think the whole point is that it's your area. He asked for your help; you were the one he wanted with him that night."

"Hey, that's right," Sam says.

"So that's what I want you to do. I want you to approach it from a forensic-accounting point of view, figure out how you could have been of help to Barry."

I turn to Hike. "You're in charge of getting Sam what he needs. Some of the financial stuff will be in discovery, some will be in Price's house, since he worked out of there. Denise can grant you access. Some of it you'll have to subpoena from the company or the prosecutor."

Back to Sam. "And just in case we miss something, you should do your computer magic."

"Hack into his company?" he asks.

I nod. "Hack away."

"You got it, boss."

"What else you got for me?" Hike asks. It's a surprising question from him, since he doesn't get paid by the hour.

"Botulism. I know you think you know a lot about it, but I want to know everything there is to know. I'm especially interested in when the poison had to be administered for Barry to have had the reaction when he did."

"No problem," Hike says. "What are you going to do?"

"Did you get the additional discovery?"

126

"Yup. That is one accommodating prosecutor. I think we could order a pizza and he'd deliver it to us. With extra anchovies."

"It won't last," I say. I had Hike request Barry's calendar and personal papers. They weren't part of the original discovery, because they are not part of the evidence that will be used against Denise. The prosecutor has an obligation to turn over only the evidence that will be part of the trial.

"I'm going to use his calendar to try and re-create his steps. Something happened to make him call Sam when he did; maybe I can figure it out that way. Sam, can you get me his phone records?"

"Sure. Home? Cell?"

"Yes and yes." Sam can hack into phone records faster than I can find an online weather forecast.

"Good," I say. "Let's do it."

Hike leaves the office and Sam says, "Andy, can I show you something?"

"What?"

"In my office. Just take a second."

He leads me down to his office and unlocks the door. In all the time I've known Sam, I've never known him to lock his office door. He opens the door slowly and quietly, and I follow him in.

He takes me to the door of his back office

127

and says softly, "Take a look."

I look in and there is Crash, sleeping soundly on a bed that Sam has constructed out of six pillows. "He's home," he says.

"He's going to live here?" I ask, just because I have a need to ask irritating questions.

"No, you know what I mean . . . he's not at the vet's office anymore."

"That's great, Sam."

"Watch this," he says, and then calls out loudly, "Crash! Hey, Crash!"

Crash's eyes open, and he lifts his head slightly to see who is annoying him by waking him up. When he sees it's Sam, who he has probably already figured out is a nutcase, he plops his head down and goes back to sleep.

"You see that?" asks Sam.

"What?"

"He knows his name."

"Or he just heard a noise and wanted to check it out."

Sam shakes his head. "No way. I'll show you." He then calls out, more softly than before, "Tara! Hey, Tara!"

Once again Crash lifts his head, checks us out, and puts his head back down.

"Wow, that's amazing," I say. "He's already learned Tara's name as well. This dog is a genius."

Sam doesn't seem to have a sense of humor when it comes to Crash. He may even think I'm serious.

"When I have something important to do or I'm worried about something, I pet him," Sam says. "He's a good-luck charm."

"I'll give it a shot," I say, and I walk over and pet Crash on the head.

"What was that for?" Sam asks.

"I bet the Knicks tonight against the Lakers. It's Crash against Kobe."

Nothing could go wrong. Mike Cardenas was reasonably confident of that. As the customs officer in charge of one section of Port Newark, this was his domain, so he was in the perfect position to make sure that things went smoothly.

That's not to say he wasn't disconcerted by his lack of knowledge of the situation, because he certainly was. He didn't even know what was in the cargo container. He had been assured it wasn't nuclear material, and the fact that the radiation detectors had not gone off thankfully confirmed that. His guess was drugs, though it could be conventional arms.

Whatever it was had to be important. Mike had already received a hundred thousand dollars for his part in the operation, with another two hundred thousand to come. For that kind of money, they weren't smuggling in chocolates.

Mike still had no idea how they found him or knew his situation. Carter wouldn't explain that or anything else. But they knew he was vulnerable, knew that he had incurred gambling debts he could not afford, knew he was desperate for money.

They knew he would go along.

Going along was easy. The shipment would come in, eighteen cargo containers from Thailand, apparently carrying kitchen appliances for a chain of stores in the Midwest. He would have three of them opened as part of a random testing process. Such a process was not conducted on all shipments; some went unopened entirely. But opening three would show diligence and responsibility, and would provide deniability.

Making sure that the key container went unopened was easy. Carter had supplied him with the serial number, so he could be positive there was no mistake.

And there was not. The shipment came in on schedule, and Mike handled it exactly as he promised he would. Three containers were opened, and they were filled with dishwashers and ranges. Nothing was amiss, and there was certainly no apparent reason for anyone doing his job to have looked further.

So Mike signed off on it, and the entire shipment cleared customs. Within three hours it was on trucks and heading for a destination that Mike did not know.

Which was fine with Mike, because he didn't want to know.

Kenneth Rebhun put on a tuxedo for our meeting. I'm not particularly flattered by the gesture. He had asked that we meet at the Palace Hotel in Manhattan because he and his wife were being honored that night for their philanthropy. Since they lived way out on Long Island, I jumped at the chance of having to drive only as far as the city to talk to him.

We meet in his suite, and he apologizes that his wife isn't quite ready to greet me, as she is in the bedroom getting dressed. He grins. "You'd think after all these years she'd have figured out how to speed up the process."

Kenneth is probably in his early sixties and has obviously spent quite a bit of time in tuxedos. Men who wear them rarely, like myself, walk around like somebody stuck a hanger up their ass, while those who wear them often seem entirely comfortable doing so.

"I appreciate your seeing me on such short notice," I say.

"I want to do anything I can to help."

"Help Denise Price?"

"Help the truth come out. Not that I think I'll be able to add much."

"I'm just beginning my investigation," I say, "but I know that Barry Price handled your investments."

He nodded. "Some of them. Close to two hundred million dollars."

I know from my research that Rebhun is the retired founder of a significant oil and gas company, and has a net worth of close to six hundred million dollars.

"Obviously you had confidence in him."

"And he repeatedly justified that confidence."

"Did you monitor the trades closely?"

"No. As I said, I had full confidence in Barry."

"And you made money?"

He nods. "Consistently."

"He met with you three days before he died," I say.

Kenneth seems surprised that I know this. "He did."

"What was that meeting about?"

There is suddenly a wariness about him that I hadn't seen before. At that moment his wife, Cathy, walks into the room. She's beautiful, very much like I imagine Laurie will look at sixty. I actually think women get more attractive as they get older, though no one I know agrees with that.

He introduces us and then resumes talking openly in front of her. "May I ask why you want to know about that meeting?"

"I want to know everything I can about Barry Price, especially in the time just before his death. It's necessary for me to defend my client."

"Look, Mr. Carpenter, Barry Price . . . well, I wouldn't say he was like a son to me, he was more like a close nephew. And I very much like Denise as well."

Cathy is nodding vigorously along with all of this.

He continues, "So I do not want to contribute to destroying his memory. He was an extraordinary individual. And brilliant."

"But you want to bring his killer to justice?"

He thinks for a moment and says, "That I do. Barry suggested that I close out my account and withdraw my investment."

"Why?"

"He didn't say, and I didn't press it, in

case there were insider issues or the like. But my sense was that he was leaving the business. I could have been wrong about that."

"Did you do what he suggested?"

"Of course. I withdrew twenty-five percent of it, as he instructed. He wanted me to do it in four installments, spread out over three months."

"Do you think Denise Price murdered her husband?"

Cathy is shaking her head no as Kenneth says, "I do not. But then again, I don't see how anyone could have done something like this."

Cathy says, "There is no way on earth that Denise did this."

"Why do you say that?" I ask, hoping she has some concrete reason I can use.

"No woman could," Cathy says.

"You'd be surprised, Cathy," is what I don't say.

"Have a nice evening," is what I do say.

Morristown Municipal Airport is a designated relief airport for the New York area. That means it was built to serve as a place for planes to go when JFK, LaGuardia, or Newark becomes overcrowded. Since I have never been at those airports when they're not overcrowded, I'm surprised that Morristown Airport is so empty.

I'm here to see John Mulligan, whom Barry Price employed to mechanically maintain his plane. Since Barry's plane is currently in about four million pieces, I expect Mulligan to have some time on his hands, but that turns out not to be the case.

Mulligan is working on a plane when I walk into the hangar, and he comes down wearing work overalls. He greets me with a smile and a handshake. His hands aren't greasy; I don't think private planes have any grease. Grease is for peasants.

"Sorry, but I need to work while we talk.

Hope you don't mind, but it's a busy week."

"So you didn't work exclusively for Barry Price?"

He smiles so broadly that it almost qualifies as a laugh, and he says no. He clearly thinks it's the dumbest question ever asked. If he hung around with me more he'd know it's not even in the top fifty for this week.

There are probably twenty planes in and around the hangar, each one way too small for me to consider getting on. It's counterintuitive; small planes scare me, even though it's harder to understand how the large ones stay in the air.

Before I can ask him questions, he has one for me. "Do you know what brought the plane down?"

"Pilot error," I say.

"Really? Barry was about as good a pilot as I work with."

"His error was that he didn't stay conscious." I don't want to mention the poison, though that will come out in the press soon enough.

"So Denise gave him something that knocked him out?"

"You know Denise?" I ask.

"Sure. She flew with Barry all the time. I'm not sure why he brought her; all they did was argue. But the plane was in perfect shape; I serviced it that day."

"Was that a regular service?"

"Every time he was taking it up. He was very careful about that."

"So he would call and say when he was flying?"

He nods. "Every time. The only thing different about this time was that he said he would be going the next day, not that night. I was surprised by that."

"Did he say where he was going?"

"Sure did. He always had me lay out a flight plan and confirm with the receiving airport that he was coming. You don't have to do all that, but like I said, he was careful."

"Where was he going that night?" I ask.

"Augusta, Maine."

"Had he ever been there before?"

Mulligan shakes his head. "He'd never flown there, at least not since I'd been working with him."

"And you had no idea why he was going?"

"Nah, he didn't tell me stuff like that. I figure it was business. I mean Maine, this time of year, it wasn't like spring break, you know?"

"How long was he going for?"

"That's the weird thing. Mr. Price, I mean he did everything on a schedule, everything was planned out. He would always tell me when he'd be back, and I could set my watch by it. But this time he didn't tell me; I remember thinking that was strange."

I'm out of questions, except for one more. I point toward one of the private jets. "How much do these things cost?"

"That one is three million five."

"Does it come with peanuts and those little pillows?"

He laughs. "All included."

"And those bags to throw up in?"

"Now you're pushing it."

What he doesn't know, and what I've just realized myself, is that I could afford one of those planes if I wanted it.

What a country.

"This is New Hampshire, for Christ's sake. Stuff like that doesn't happen here."

The reaction by Governor Neil Romano was pretty much what FBI Agent Muñoz expected. But he had an obligation to report what he knew and to strongly make security suggestions.

"What about four murders in a gas station, Governor? What about the cold-blooded killing of an undercover police officer? Does that happen in New Hampshire?"

The murder of Drew Keller and three other men was as sensational a crime as New Hampshire had seen in years, so Governor Romano knew exactly what Muñoz was talking about.

Muñoz had brought State Police Chief Gerald Krespi to drive home the point, and Krespi had predicted that the message would not be well received. But since Krespi was entrusted with the governor's pro-

tection, he was prepared to be very persua-
sive.

Romano, in office for fewer than four
months, was a gruff seat-of-the-pants executive who had quickly developed a reputation for speaking well in advance of thinking. That style had already earned him a
number of enemies, both in and out of the
legislature. He presented himself as a man
of the people, often literally walking around
town, hanging out in restaurants, and talking to citizens.

"Governor, these people spoke about an
assassination. They were themselves murdered, which adds some credibility to their
statements, don't you think?"

"There is no evidence that they are after
me," Romano said.

"Maybe not," Muñoz said. "But we just
had a presidential campaign, so candidates
won't be here for three years. This is New
Hampshire, Governor. It's not exactly a
target-rich environment for political big
shots. Right now you're as big as it gets."

Romano turned to Krespi. "So protect
me."

"We'll do that. But you will need to take
extra precautions."

"I'm going to live a normal life."

Muñoz was losing patience. "You're not

normal. You're the governor. By definition there is only one of you in the entire state. So you are not normal, and you are definitely not bulletproof."

"So what do you propose?"

"I propose that until we get a resolution on this, you listen to him," Muñoz said, pointing to Krespi. "If he doesn't think something you're planning is safe, you don't do it. Stay in the bubble."

"I don't like this," Romano said, but it was clear that he was weakening.

"It will be for only as long as the threat exists," Krespi said.

They discussed Romano's upcoming travel plans, viewing the most dangerous times as when he was on the road, out of the executive mansion. There was to be a governors' conference in Iowa, and then a northeastern version in Augusta, Maine.

"We'll augment the normal security when you're traveling, Governor. That's standard procedure."

The meeting ended with general agreement on how to proceed, though neither Krespi nor Muñoz had full confidence that Romano was on board. They would have to monitor his movements very carefully, at least until they removed the danger.

What they did not realize was that there was no danger at all.

Tara likes Crash, and the feeling seems to be mutual. That's a good thing, if Sam is ever going to come to my house again. Because he goes absolutely nowhere without his lucky lifesaving, heaven-sent, superterrific dog.

He's come over this evening to go over the work he's done, and after some obligatory sniffing of private parts, Crash and Tara settle down on dog beds for naps. Crash is really big on naps; it's staying awake that he doesn't seem particularly fond of.

Based on the bedraggled condition he was in when Sam hit him, and the calluses on his elbows, Crash has not had an easy life. But he's retired now and seems determined to enjoy it. Good for him; he deserves it.

In any event, both he and Tara are too mature, and have been around the block too many times, to start running around or wrestling.

Before we get into what Sam has found out with his computer work, the doorbell rings. Laurie yells out that she'll get it. I can't see who is there when she opens the door, but I can hear the raised voices. Not raised angry, but raised excited and pleased.

"Look who's here, Andy," Laurie says as she walks toward us, so I do. And what I see are none other than Morris Fishman, Leon Goldberg, and the Mandlebaums, Hilda and Eli.

They are Sam's prize pupils at a computer class he teaches at the Wayne YMHA. The youngest among them is probably eighty, the tallest among them, Morris, is maybe five five, and the least energetic among them, Eli, makes me look comatose.

Hilda hugs me hello, but the three men just slap me on the arm. They don't hold back with Laurie, however; she gets hugged like crazy. All of them then shower affection on Tara and Crash.

Sam walks over and talks softly to me without them hearing. "You don't mind that I have the whole team on this, do you?"

Sam swears that they are dynamite on the computer, and the truth is they were a big help on a recent case. "The more the merrier," I say.

"Good. We've got two adjoining rooms at

the Holiday Inn on Route 4, where we're set up. Hilda calls it 'the bunker.' "

The last time I saw them, there were five of them, but Stanley Rubinstein is not here. "Where's Stanley?" I ask, regretting the question as soon as it leaves my mouth.

"He's not with us anymore," says Morris.

"Oh. I'm sorry," I say, but Hilda chimes in with "Dummy went to Florida. He calls every week. You should hear him go on about the clubhouse and the shows . . ."

"You would think he invented shuffle-board," Eli says.

"Where's Marcus?" asks Hilda. Marcus had met this group on the last case. "He's funny."

"Yeah, he's a riot. I think he's performing at the Improv tonight."

I finally get everybody focused on the matter at hand. Sam and his team have gotten a list of clients for the Price Group, and it roughly matches the one that Mark Clemens provided. About forty percent of the clients are private individuals, and the rest are companies.

"You want us to do background work on the investors?" Sam asks.

I nod. "Please. I want to know who they are, how long they've had their money with the company, how they've done on their investments, and anything else that stands out. Is that possible?"

"Sure. In the meantime, you want to go over the phone list?"

Sam has gotten Barry's home and cell phone records for the last two weeks of his life, and I very much want to go over them.

Laurie walks into the room and asks everybody if they want some coffee. Eli, Hilda, and Sam all think that sounds great. "And maybe a biscuit for Crash?" Laurie asks.

"What kind of biscuits do you have?" Sam asks.

"Milk-Bone," Laurie says.

"Store-bought?"

"No, we opened a biscuit plant in our basement," I say.

Sam informs us that he has found some recipes online and bakes his own dog biscuits. He takes a couple out of his briefcase, and they look so good I wouldn't mind trying one myself. He gives one to Crash and one to Tara. It turns out that Crash is so smart he's able to eat a biscuit with his eyes closed.

We go over the phone lists. Sam has put down names and addresses for each of the numbers. Most of them are New York listings or ones near the Price home in Jersey.

I'll ask Laurie to track them all down, but I'm not overly hopeful.

One number that does attract my interest is that of Donald Susser. It includes the area code 207, and the address Sam has is in Waldoboro, Maine.

"Do you know if that's near Augusta?"

Sam shrugs and says, "Let me check." He goes to his computer, types something, and maybe thirty seconds later says, "It's about twenty-five miles away."

I look at the list and see that Barry had called the number three times, all during the week before he died. The last call had been made the morning of the crash.

"Barry was flying to Augusta that night," I say.

"How do you know that?"

"I'm a trained investigator. Can you find out anything about Susser?"

Sam goes online and within minutes is able to tell me how old he is, that he was married for two years but is now divorced, is ex-army, has a DUI on his record, and until six weeks ago was collecting unemployment insurance. There's a bunch more detail as well; it's a remarkable performance.

I call the number and a young woman answers on the first ring with a "Hello?" that sounds sort of hopeful, as if she were waiting for a call. She'll no doubt be disappointed that it's me, keeping alive a streak of female reactions that I've had happen to me since high school.

"I'd like to speak to Donald Susser."

"Who is this?" I'm surprised that her tone sounds more wary than disappointed.

"My name is Andy Carpenter; I'm an attorney in New Jersey. I need to talk to him about a case I have."

"What kind of case?"

"Is Mr. Susser there? I really must speak to him directly."

"He's not here."

"What time do you expect him back?"

"He's not coming back."

The Andy Carpenter Female Mood Detector tells me that this woman is nervous, scared, and sad. Usually I'm right one out of three times, which in this case would still be significant. "Can you give him a message?"

"Maybe. I don't know."

"I'd really appreciate it if you could. Tell him that an attorney named Andy Carpenter called, and please ask him to call me back on an important matter about Barry Price." Then I give her my phone number, and by instinct, I throw in, "I think I can provide him the help he needs."

"I won't be talking to him."

"If you give him the message, you'll be doing something very good for him."

I get off the phone and describe the conversation to Laurie and Sam, and we discuss all the ways the woman's tone and Susser's being unavailable likely have nothing whatsoever to do with Barry Price.

"I'd still like to talk to him," I say.

Sam walks over to Crash and pets him on the head. "Andy needs some help, old buddy," he says. "He wants to talk to this guy Susser."

None of the group wants to stay for dinner. Sam plans to take Crash through the drive-thru at McDonald's, and it's getting close to bedtime for his geriatric assistants. They all leave, and I order in a pizza, half extra cheese for me, and half with all kinds of disgustingly healthy vegetables on it for Laurie. The crust is Tara's domain.

Laurie wants to have a glass of wine, always a good sign as bedtime nears but not really conclusive. When we're finished, we head up to the bedroom.

"Sam is crazy about that dog," she says.

" 'Crazy' is definitely the operative word," I say. "Although the Knicks did beat the Lakers last night."

"I don't understand."

"Sam told me that if I petted Crash, I'd win my bet on the Knicks. It worked out."

"You don't believe in that kind of superstition."

I am the furthest thing from a superstitious person. "Of course not. Do you?"

"I say go with what works. And Crash seems to be working quite well."

"What do you mean?"

"Well, he saved Sam's life, the Knicks won, and you petted him when he came in tonight."

"So?"

She smiles. "So you're about to get lucky."

Spreading out across the country was the time when the risk was greatest. That was Carter's view, and it is what he conveyed to his superior. It had been necessary to bring them all to the upstate New York base of operations, but then getting them to their individual assignments was a complicated, and relatively dangerous, process.

Each man traveled with professionally prepared fake documentation that should have no trouble standing up to local law enforcement scrutiny. They drove cars registered to their assumed names, with up-to-date insurance and inspection stickers.

The men traveled in pairs; that was essential to their work. And they were well trained. There was no chance that they might do something foolish to attract attention.

But the dangers remained, and they were impossible to predict. There could be a traffic accident, perhaps the fault of another driver. Or maybe they would be stopped by the police for another reason altogether, perhaps even a mistaken identity. But the worst thing that could happen, though Carter could not imagine a credible scenario in which it would occur, would be a cop getting a look at what was in the trunk of each car.

But one thing Carter and his superior were sure of: the men were thoroughly loyal. If somehow taken into custody, they would not betray their comrades-in-arms, and the danger would thus remain isolated.

Carter had made a mistake in trying to expand the operation by hiring local talent, like the clowns in Maine and New Hampshire. It had proved to be a debacle, and the cleanup was messy.

But ultimately there was no great harm done. The scope of the operation had to be scaled down, but it remained plenty large enough. And the beauty of it was that any one part could be excised without seriously harming the big picture. That had already been demonstrated in the two New England states.

Once people were in place, the only remaining worry would be the lawyer in New Jersey, who had been sticking his nose into everything. He was proving to be a bigger problem than the FBI.

Consideration was given to eliminating him, but it was considered unwise. It would attract very substantial, and certainly unwanted, media attention, and that negative would outweigh the positive. But the decision was temporary and was subject to revision as events dictated.

Carter was under orders to achieve one hundred percent success, but that was only a goal. He knew that seventy percent would be a huge triumph and would have reverberations that would last for many decades.

Revenge was going to be extraordinarily sweet.

I like to visit clients in prison as often as possible. Actually, that's not true. It's more accurate to say that I hate to visit clients in prison. But I do it frequently, because I know what it means to them.

Denise Price, like every other person in her situation, is feeling scared and abandoned. Even worse, she's feeling helpless. She has no control of her situation and, unless I update her, doesn't even know what is going on.

As her attorney, her lifeline, just my presence reassures her that there is someone working on her behalf and trying to help her.

The downside, of course, is that my arrival triggers unrealistic expectations. She gets herself to believe that it's possible I'm bringing the magic bullet that will get her the hell out of here, and when she finds out I haven't done that, the disappointment is palpable.

I've been disappointing all kinds of women for a really long time, but for some reason I hate letting down accused murderers the most.

Of course I experience some disappointment of my own. I'm always somewhat hopeful that the client will remember a little nugget that will help in my investigation, and it rarely happens. It certainly doesn't happen today. Denise has nothing to offer in that regard.

I ask her if she's ever heard the name Donald Susser, or if she has any idea why Barry would have been going to Maine. In both cases the answer is no.

After about thirty minutes of letting each other down, I say good-bye, with the promise that I'll return as soon as I can so I can crush her hopes once again.

On the way out I pick up my cell phone, since visitors are required to check them before they can see inmates. The authorities obviously believe that without this precaution there would be a lot of prisoners escaping by phoning their way to freedom. The ironic thing is that it's widely known that there are more contraband cell phones in the prison than there are prisoners.

There are two messages from Laurie, asking me to call her as soon as I can. "Are you on the way home?" she asks when I reach her.

"Yes."

"Good. Crash's luck continues; we heard from Donald Susser."

When I get home, Marcus is in the kitchen and Laurie is feeding him. It's like feeding Shamu, with a couple of minor differences. Shamu ate only fish; Marcus will eat anything. And Marcus could kick Shamu's ass.

Laurie mentions that she had called Marcus because she wants him to hear about the Susser conversation as well. That means something dangerous is involved, something she doesn't think I can handle on my own. She's usually right.

"He's scared and he's hiding," Laurie says. "He's sure that if they find him, they'll kill him."

"Who are 'they'?"

"He wouldn't tell me that. He doesn't trust me — or you, for that matter — but he has nowhere else to turn."

"Why doesn't he go to the police?" I ask. Marcus hasn't said a word; his mouth is too full. I can only assume he's heard what Laurie's been saying, since as far as I know he doesn't have any food stuffed in his ears.

"Because he's afraid of going to jail. Andy,

I think he's interested in you as a lawyer, that maybe you can get the police to give him some kind of immunity."

"From what type of prosecution?"

"Again, he wouldn't say. But he wants to talk to you in person."

"Here?"

"No, in Maine. He gave me a specific time and place. And he insists that you come alone. Otherwise he won't talk to you."

"When does he want to meet?"

"Tomorrow evening at seven. Assuming you want to do this, you and Marcus can take a morning flight."

"No way. If he says alone, it has to be alone." I point to Marcus. "Besides, he won't have finished dinner by then."

Laurie has it all figured out. Marcus will go with me, but we'll take different planes, just in case. Then we'll each rent our own car, and he will go scout out the location for the meeting in advance. He'll be in place if there's any reason to cancel the meeting or to intervene if something goes wrong.

"We can't afford to blow this; it's our only lead," I say.

"Andy, there's a fact pattern for us to look at. And the fact is that the last person to fly to Maine to see Donald Susser is dead."

She's making a leap here. We don't know

for certain that Barry Price was going to see Donald Susser. But I understand her point, and while I continue to resist, I don't do so too strenuously. Marcus has saved my ass too many times for me to pretend it doesn't need frequent saving.

We plan our strategy. Marcus will take an eight o'clock flight, and I'll be on the ten thirty. He will both call and text me if there is any reason to abort the plan, right up until the last minute.

Situations like this are way out of my comfort zone, and it's fair to say that if I'm about to do something that requires Marcus, I shouldn't be doing it in the first place.

But Marcus's ability to protect has always been flawless in the past, which is the main reason I am alive enough to still need protection. And I definitely need something to jump-start our case; I just hope that Susser provides it.

Now if Marcus will just stop eating and get the hell out of here, I'll find out if my going to Maine for the day entitles me to going-away sex.

Portland has my idea of a great airport. It's modern, spacious, and uncrowded, with signs that actually point you in the right direction and people who smile a lot. The bags come off within five minutes, and the rental car companies are actually in the terminal. This is unlike JFK and Newark, where the rental cars are so far away they feel like they should have their own airport.

I take the highway toward Augusta, and I have to stop a few times to pay tolls. Each of the toll collectors greet me with pleasantries like "Good morning" and "How's your day going?" As I leave, they all tell me to "Have a nice day."

It was a short flight, but have I flown to a different planet? It's cold, these people are sitting in open tollbooths all day doing a boring job, and they couldn't be cheerier and friendlier. The nicest comment I ever got from a New York tollbooth collector was

"Ain't you got anything smaller?"

Marcus calls me while I'm driving, and when I answer, he says, "Yunh."

I haven't picked up on all the nuances of Marcus-talk, even after all these years, so I say, "Marcus?"

That may not have been a specific enough question, because it draws another "Yunh."

"Are we good?"

"Good," he says, and I'm relieved that we're good and that I understood what he said.

"Good," I say.

"Good," Marcus says, since once he latches onto a word he can't seem to stop using it.

In an effort to break the "good" streak, I say, "I'll see you later," and he hangs up. Talking to Marcus makes me nervous, so the end of the conversation causes me to say out loud, to myself, "Good."

I've got plenty of time to kill, so I check the map and see that there's a town called Damariscotta about twenty minutes from the meeting place. I get there at about one thirty and find a pub called King Eider's, in the middle of a quintessential New England town.

The atmosphere in the place is terrific; everybody seems to know and like everybody else. There are hundreds of mugs hanging from the ceiling, and apparently the owner of each mug is a member of some kind of drinking and eating club. I can think of worse clubs to belong to.

I have a terrific lunch and hang around for an hour and a half. I'd like to stay longer, but don't want to call attention to myself. I walk around the town for a while, then stop in the Maine Coast Book Shop & Café for coffee and a great muffin.

All in all, it would be a perfect afternoon, if not for the fact that I have a meeting coming up at which I am concerned that I could be killed.

There's always something . . .

Marcus arrived at the meeting location in the late morning. It was next to a remarkable place called Peaslee's, a combination gas station, convenience store, delicatessen, liquor store, and do-it-yourself car wash in Jefferson. One could live for years and never leave Peaslee's.

The instructions had been for Andy to be in a vacant building on a piece of land behind the store at 7:00 P.M. It was not a heavily trafficked area and was likely the kind of place where strangers would be noticed. Of course, Marcus would stand out in Giants Stadium during a playoff game, a fact that he was aware of. So he stopped there briefly, put some gas in his car, and bought some food. His goal was simply to get the lay of the land, and he did that.

He drove around the back and took a road up behind a hill. It gave him a straight line of sight, which was enhanced by binoculars.

He could see everybody arriving at the place and certainly would know when anyone went around to the back.

But based on the layout, which neither he, Andy, nor Laurie had known about the previous night, Marcus was concerned. He'd be able to tell when someone showed up and whether that person was alone. But he would not be able to tell whether he was armed or what his intentions were.

If Susser came with a weapon, for example, there would be no way Marcus could intervene in time. So he was going to change the plan. He would wait until Susser and Andy were together and then move up close, where he could impact events in his rather aggressive way.

He also had no idea what Susser looked like, but when a car pulled up at six thirty and a man got out, Marcus had little doubt it was him. The reflected light off the store and gas station area showed a young man, maybe twenty-five years old, who looked around warily before going toward the back.

Marcus memorized the license plate on the car, utilizing a tiny part of a near photographic memory that almost no one knew he possessed. Andy wasn't due to arrive for a half hour, but since Susser was obviously there, Marcus decided to move up closer to be in a position to intervene. He could do so without Susser seeing him, because he was already inside the building.

So Marcus drove down the hill to get to a closer lookout, from where he could approach the building on foot. There was an area that was fairly heavily wooded and would therefore afford him concealment.

Driving down removed the building from Marcus's line of sight for about three minutes, and when he got to his new position, he saw immediately that the game had changed. Another car had pulled up, though he didn't see any new people. Therefore, the passengers in the new car had most likely already gone into the building.

Marcus couldn't be positive that the new car wasn't Andy's rental, though he hoped and believed that it was not. Andy was under strict instructions not to arrive until seven o'clock, and it would be uncharacteristic for him to have changed the plan.

But the other side had definitely changed the plan. Andy was expecting to meet with one person, and there was certainly more than that in there now. Marcus had no idea what that meant, but he didn't want Andy walking into that building the way things stood.

Maybe Susser was one of the people in

the building, maybe not. At that point it really didn't matter to Marcus. There was no way of figuring out the ramifications of the new arrivals, but it clearly didn't jibe with Laurie's description of Susser as being alone and afraid.

He looked in the window and saw three men, including the man Marcus had believed to be Susser. They were standing close together and just talking, but it seemed fairly intense, and "Susser" was shaking his head no.

Marcus went around to the door and quietly turned the knob. It was unlocked, which made things easier. Marcus opted not to take out his gun; he didn't expect he would need it, and at this point there was no reason to kill anyone.

Displaying amazing swiftness, he opened and pushed through the door. To the three men inside, it seemed as if he exploded into the room. If they backed off, Marcus would not hurt them but rather find out what the hell was going on.

They didn't back off. After a moment of initial surprise, the two newcomers to the room moved toward Marcus, one of them reaching into his jacket pocket for what Marcus decided to assume was a weapon.

He grabbed that man's arm and snapped

it at the wrist, then picked up the screaming man and threw him, full body, at his partner. The flying man was the bigger of the two, so he collapsed the smaller man and they landed in a pile.

Marcus quickly frisked and took a handgun from each of the fallen men. He turned and took a quick look at the man he figured was Susser. He appeared shocked and scared but did not make any threatening gestures, so Marcus didn't touch him.

Which was just as well, because it was time to talk.

The meeting doesn't exactly follow my planned agenda. I figured it would be just Susser and me, and he would tell me why he was afraid and what it had to do with Barry Price. I'd help him if I could, if he deserved that help, and then I'd go home to put the information I learned to good use defending my client.

Instead, when I get there, Marcus is in the room with three men, and the place looks like a bomb went off in it. One of the men is holding his arm at an awkward angle and moaning; people moan a lot around Marcus. Another man looks somewhat dazed and out of it, another Marcus trademark.

The three men glance at me briefly, but their real focus is on Marcus. It's a very logical attitude for them to take.

"What's going on, guys?" I ask, and Marcus nods to the unharmed man, which serves as a clear instruction for him to answer. But he hesitates.

"Are you Donald Susser?" I ask. It's an educated guess; he's unshaven and wearing dirty jeans and a flannel shirt that looks like he hasn't taken it off since the first Clinton administration. He also looks scared, though with his having just seen Marcus in action, that's not exactly a surprise.

He nods. "Yes."

"Who are these two?"

"They're my friends. That's Billy Jordan and that's Teddy Ellis." Ellis is the one with the broken arm.

"You said we'd be alone. Why are they here?"

"They were sent to kill me," Susser says, and Ellis shakes his head weakly in disagreement.

"Sounds like really good friends," I say. "Why were they sent to kill you, and who sent them?"

"We told him everything," Susser says, meaning Marcus.

If I have to get the story out of Marcus, I should have it by the time of Denise Price's third or fourth parole hearing. "I want to hear it from you," I say.

So he tells me that a man named Carter had hired them to commit a murder, though he called it an assassination. He claims they

170

didn't know who the target was, that Carter hadn't told them yet. But they were each going to get two hundred thousand dollars for their efforts.

"Why did this Carter pick you three?"

Susser nods toward Jordan. "Because Billy was army artillery; Carter put him in charge."

"What kind of weapon?"

"We weren't told yet."

I ask a bunch more questions, mostly about Carter, but he seems to be pretty much a mystery man. They could be withholding something, though Marcus usually extracts all there is to extract. Susser does say that his two friends were supposed to kill him for talking to Barry Price, which made him a threat to the operation. But he swears they weren't going to actually do it. They were just going to tell Carter that he was dead and hide him until after things quieted down.

"Why was Barry Price coming here?" I ask.

"I don't know."

"You didn't call him?"

He shakes his head. "He called me, said he wanted to talk. That's how all this started."

I ask Marcus if he thinks there's more to

be gotten from the three, and he shakes his head. So we let them go, which seems to be something they're rather happy about.

I decide that we should spend the night in Maine. This is not exactly a tough call. First of all, there are no more flights out of Portland tonight, so the alternative is to spend seven hours in a car with Marcus. It's not the worst thing imaginable — Hike would be worse — but it's pretty bad.

But more important, I'm not leaving without talking to law enforcement about Donald Susser and his friends. If there really is to be a murder committed, by them or someone else, it's information that I can't sit on.

Marcus and I check into the Senator Inn, on Western Avenue in Augusta, and we head straight for their restaurant. They sell shrimp cocktail by the piece, and when the waiter asks Marcus how many he wants, he thinks for a moment and then says, "Thirty."

"Thirty?" asks the waiter.

I nod. "He doesn't want to spoil his appetite for dinner."

I'm ready to go to my room an hour later, just about the time Marcus is starting on his third entrée, so I tell the waiter to charge the meal to my room. "The whole thing?" he asks.

I nod. "It's fine; I took out a mortgage on the meal." When I get back to the room I fall asleep immediately. It's been a tiring and mostly wasted day.

In the morning, I head to the restaurant. Marcus is in there eating; for all I know he's been at it all night. I tell him my plan, such as it is, which is to head for the local police to tell them at least part of what I know.

The nearest precinct is just a short drive from the hotel. I debate whether or not to have Marcus come in with me and decide that he should, though my plan is to do the talking. I don't discuss this with Marcus first, since asking Marcus not to talk seems a tad unnecessary.

I tell the sergeant at the front desk that I have some information about a local resident named Donald Susser, who might be involved in criminal activity. I put it that way for a couple of reasons. In my experience, cops prefer to receive information rather than answer questions, and "criminal activity" is something that they have an instinctive interest in.

Whatever I said, it works. The sergeant says, "Give me a second," then picks up the phone and talks softly into it. Less than a minute later, another officer comes out and takes us back to the office of Captain Luther Ketchell.

We introduce ourselves, but he barely looks at me; his focus is on Marcus. Finally he says, "Talk to me about Donald Susser."

I lay it out for him, from Barry Price's murder, to my representation of Denise, to the connection to Donald Susser and his phone conversation with Laurie, to the situation at Peaslee's with Susser, Jordan, and Ellis, and finally to the murder they have apparently been hired to commit. Pretty much the only thing I leave out is the forceful means that Marcus used to get the information. "I thought you should know all this," I say.

Ketchell thinks about this for a few long moments and then says, "Good thinking. Too bad you didn't come in a little earlier."

"Why is that?"

"Susser, Jordan, and Ellis are dead. They were found in Damariscotta State Park last night with one bullet in each of their heads. Lying side by side, staring at the moon."

Ketchell decides there's no way he can let

us leave there without completely debriefing us on everything we know but may not yet have revealed. To do so, he separates Marcus and me so we can be questioned separately. It's the first break I've gotten all day; watching them try to get answers out of Marcus would be too painful to witness.

After almost four hours, we're finally told that we can go but that we might be hearing from Homeland Security. Protocol calls for Ketchell to contact them once the word "assassination" was raised.

We get a four o'clock flight out of Portland. It was a very worthwhile trip, except for the part where we lost our only promising lead, and the three people we talked to all got killed.

Everything's really going according to plan.

The system is set up to work against us. I think it is pretty clear already that our main hope is to prove that Denise is not guilty, or at least credibly point to someone else as the killer. We will obviously also try to create reasonable doubt as to Denise's guilt, but it's unlikely that will be enough.

The situation in Maine leads me to believe very strongly that Denise did not murder her husband. Having met Susser and studied his background, I am sure that he was not someone Barry would have had investment business with. It seems far more likely that he was somehow involved in the reason that Barry needed a criminal attorney.

I have no way of knowing why Barry called Susser and then arranged to see him. They lived in different worlds, geographically and financially, and it is crucial that we find out Barry's motive for making the connection.

The fact that Susser, Jordan, and Ellis were killed, and so soon after Barry's murder, makes the coincidence way too great for me to believe all the deaths are unrelated. And of course it's unlikely that Denise broke out of prison to murder Susser and his friends.

But there are evidentiary rules in a trial, much as I like to break them. For us to bring in outside evidence, such as Susser's death, we need to show relevance. That is always difficult to do, and in this case will be even tougher.

Laurie and I are taking Tara for a walk when she says, "I wonder how they found Susser."

I ask her to explain, and she says, "He was scared and obviously in hiding. Yet the other two guys knew where he was going to be and when he was going to be there."

"They weren't necessarily bad guys; they were apparently his friends. Don't forget, they're just as dead as he is."

She shakes her head. "But he was in hiding from everyone. If they knew where he was, they wouldn't have had to show up at your meeting to find him. They could have done so at any time."

"An excellent observation," I admit.

"Somehow they knew in advance that he

was going to be there, and based on how he sounded on the phone, I doubt that he told them."

"Susser said that this guy Carter sent them to kill him. Carter must have been the one who knew about our meeting. Maybe Susser's phone was tapped."

She shook her head. "You have to know where somebody is to tap his phone. Unless . . ."

She doesn't have to finish the sentence. It's crazy, but I know that she's considering the possibility that our phone is the one that is tapped. "You have someone who can check it out?" I ask.

"Of course. Tony Vazquez is the best."

"He won't find anything," I say.

"That would be the preferred outcome."

"Call him."

She nods.

It sounds like somebody is screaming in the background when Sam answers the phone. "What the hell is that?" I ask.

"Rage Against the Machine."

I have no idea how I know that Rage Against the Machine is a band, but I do. And I also know that Sam's idea of a wild night out is seeing *Fiddler on the Roof* at the dinner theater.

"Your taste in music is evolving," I say.

"Crash likes alternative rock. It mellows him right out."

"Then he must have a lot of it on his iPod, because he's the most mellow dog I've ever seen."

"Externally, yes. But inside he has a lot of stress. And he's been through a lot — the accident, the surgery . . ."

I take a moment to silently give thanks that Tara likes Simon and Garfunkel, and then I say, "I need you to do something today, unless you're taking Crash to a Metallica concert."

"No, I'm on the case."

"Okay. I want you to dig into the lives of three guys who lived in Augusta. Their names are Donald Susser, Billy Jordan, and Teddy Ellis."

He already knew Susser's name, but he pauses as he writes down the others. "Okay, good. I'm heading down to the bunker now."

"The bunker?"

"Yeah, you remember, at the Holiday Inn. That's where the team is."

"Right. How are they doing?"

"Great. Hilda's upset that room service doesn't have potato latkes, but other than that it's going really well. What do you want to know about the Augusta guys?"

"Everything. Employment, family, criminal record if they have one, financial dealings. Anything you can hack into will help."

"And they all live in Augusta proper?"

"I'm not sure 'live' is the verb that applies anymore, but that's the general area where they're from."

He promises to get right on it, and I head out to interview some of Denise and Barry's friends, a number of whom are on the prosecution's witness list.

181

It's a depressing afternoon. Each of the people I speak with is in retrospect well aware of Denise and Barry's marital problems and not totally surprised that things ended in violence. I don't believe them; they are all employing twenty-twenty hindsight.

I don't come on strong with them, just listen to what they have to say. I'll be seeing some of them on the witness stand, and I certainly don't want them to consider me a particular threat going in.

When I get home, there's a car that I don't recognize in the driveway. I get out of my car and see that Laurie has come out on the porch to greet me. She's obviously missed me terribly, the poor thing.

"We need to talk," she says.

"Uh-oh."

"Tony Vazquez is inside."

For a second the name doesn't connect to anything, but then I remember that he's the security guy who's a friend of Laurie's and who was going to check the phone for bugs.

"So why are we out here?"

"He's coming right out."

The door opens as she finishes the sentence, and he appears on cue. Laurie introduces us, and then he gets right to it. "Your phone is compromised," he says. "Somebody is listening to every word you say."

"You're sure?"

"Positive. It's a very sophisticated device; you're dealing with professionals."

"How professional?"

"Let's put it this way: there are governments that don't have access to this kind of stuff."

"Was somebody in the house?"

"Not for this; the device is off premises."

"So why are we talking out here?"

"Tony hasn't checked the house for bugs or cameras yet," Laurie says, "so I figured it's best we talk out here, just in case."

"Did you leave the tap on the phone?"

He nods. "I did. There's no way they would know that you know about it."

"Unless there are cameras in the house, and they saw you checking it out."

"Right."

Tony goes back in to finish his work, and Laurie and I go in as well. He is incredibly thorough and takes three more hours to completely check out everything in the house.

"You're clean," he says and heads down to the office to find out if the phone there has been similarly compromised. I call Hike on my cell phone and ask him to be there to let Tony in.

When he leaves, Laurie and I discuss the

latest developments. These conversations are important to me; talking about things out loud helps crystallize my thoughts.

They apparently have crystallized Laurie's as well. "Barry was obviously into something very deep and very dangerous. And now you are in the middle of it."

"No question about it."

"Which means Denise Price is innocent."

I nod. "All I have to do is prove it."

The office phone is also compromised. Tony Vazquez called Laurie on her cell phone to tell her. It presents us with an opportunity. The fact that we know somebody is listening means that we can control what he hears.

This situation causes me to have a number of conflicting emotions. The invasion of privacy is infuriating, and even though I have no idea who is doing it, I make a silent vow to get revenge when I find out.

It's also revealing, in what it says about Denise's situation. Because she is my only client, there's no doubt that whoever is listening is related to Denise's case. Although I really don't need any further confirmation after the murders in Augusta, this provides it.

Dangerous people are watching.

All of the events are more than a little scary. If Susser and the others were killed just to prevent them from talking first to Barry Price and then to me, I have to be at least a little concerned about my own safety. Since I was born without a courage gene, I'm not feeling too good about this.

Pretty much the only positive to be found in all this is that if the bad guys have been listening in on the office phone, they've had to suffer through Edna's conversations. For instance, the other day she spent an hour and a half talking to her cousin Cecelia about the upcoming crossword tournament.

I heard only a portion of Edna's side of the call, and I wanted to scream. If someone had to listen to both sides of the entire conversation, my guess is he would have preferred to be waterboarded.

I give it careful thought and make the decision to have the taps removed. Tony Vazquez had said he could do so easily, though of course whoever is listening in will be aware we discovered the taps and got rid of them.

I don't want to worry about what we say on our phones, and I can't control what callers say to us. I'm giving up the chance to set a trap by saying what we want the bad guys to hear, but there's a good chance we might never spring that trap anyway.

Sam comes in with his initial report on

the investors in Barry Price's fund. I had asked him to find out who they are, in as much detail as he could. He's not happy with the results.

"About sixty percent of the money is easy to trace," he says. "They're big-time investors, pension funds, that kind of thing. The other forty percent is not so easy."

"Why not?"

"It's all foreign companies; Cayman Islands, Belize, Barbados, Switzerland . . ."

"Tax shelter stuff?"

"Maybe, but I don't think so. We're not talking about big-time companies; I haven't even heard of any of them. I'm checking them out, but I think this money has been hiding under a rock."

"Laundering?"

He shrugs. "Could be."

"So let's think this through and assume it's laundering," I say. "Foreign entities were laundering money through Barry's company, and he found out about it. He wanted to understand it better, so he needed a financial guy outside his company he could trust."

Sam nods. "So he called me."

"Right. And he was afraid he might have legal jeopardy if he revealed it, so he was interested in a criminal attorney."

"Makes perfect sense."

"So why was he going to see Susser?"

"Maybe Susser was going to be on the receiving end of some of the money, as payment for the murder he was going to commit."

"How would Barry know that?"

"Barry was smart."

"Too bad he's not around. He could help us solve his own murder."

"I think we got something here, Andy. Hilda said it and she was right: those foreign companies are going to lead us to the answer."

"Maybe. Or maybe those companies will just turn out to be rich people hiding their money so they can stay rich."

Some people believe Homeland Security is an uncoordinated mess. They think that the right hand does not know what the left hand is doing. This is as a result of anecdotal mistakes, sometimes comical, that are then publicized. Two-year-olds are stopped from flying because they're on the terrorist watch list, wrong houses are raided . . . the list goes on.

The truth is the communication among departments is good approaching excellent, and getting better all the time. It's a vast bureaucracy but not nearly as unwieldy as commonly assumed and capable of swift and coordinated action.

Thus it was that within hours after Luther Ketchell reported to Homeland Security that Susser and his pals had talked to Andy Carpenter about a possible assassination, the information was funneled to the FBI.

Eight hours later, that same information

found its way to the office of Special Agent Ricardo Muñoz, at that time on temporary assignment in Concord, New Hampshire. Muñoz had been assigned to investigate the murder of undercover police officer Drew Keller, because the specter of assassination had come up in that case as well.

Muñoz did not consider it likely that the two cases were related. The Augusta, Maine, case was limited to an accounting by a lawyer that the victim mentioned the word "assassination." It was most likely a botched case of murder for hire.

But there were two possible connections that made it worth following up on. One was that both cases were in small northeastern cities that happened to be state capitals, and the other was that the suspected assassins were themselves murdered.

One of the negative aspects of good communication among government agencies is the overwhelming amount of that communication. Agents are often flooded with information that could conceivably relate to the cases they are working on, and full attention cannot be paid to each situation.

So the information bit that related to the murders in Augusta was relegated to near the bottom of the investigative totem pole. One of Muñoz's assistants would at some point analyze it and decide if it was actually worth following up on.

But that would not be any time soon.

A trial date is like a car in a passenger door mirror . . . it's always closer than you think. Denise's insistence on a speedy trial complicates matters, but really not that much. The trial could start three years from Wednesday, and I wouldn't think it was enough time.

The case against her is strong but primarily circumstantial. The Prices were known to have a troubled marriage, one that she wanted out of. Her previous job as a pharmaceutical assistant likely gave her the ability to make the poison, and her being in the house with Barry certainly gave her the opportunity to administer it.

I'm operating on two tracks. One is to prepare Denise's defense against the testimony that the prosecution's witnesses will offer. That is an area that I am comfortable with; it's what I do. I certainly wish I had more ammunition with which to do it, but I can be fairly resourceful in compensating for that.

The other area is at least as important but much less in my control. Barry Price's business dealings with his foreign investors are proving difficult for Sam and his team to penetrate. That difficulty is frustrating but at the same time tends to confirm my view that there is something to be found. It is something that I believe relates directly to Barry's murder.

Tonight is like every other night in trial preparation. I've spent hours going over the discovery documents and witness reports. It's at least the fifth time I've read each piece of material, which probably represents only half the times I will eventually do so.

I need to know everything cold, so that when something comes up at trial my mind will be like a file cabinet from which I can retrieve all relevant information. I have to avoid what often happened when I would call a girl in high school, which means that I can't reflect back on a cross-examination and say, "Damn, I wish I had thought to say that."

Before I go to sleep I decide to go on the computer and do my own research on some of the issues at trial. I'll have an expert witness on botulism, but my own sources of knowledge can't hurt.

After I do that unproductively for a while, I check my e-mails and discover something simultaneously shocking yet pleasing. I obviously underestimate my fame and, to be brutally honest, my sex appeal, and this is a perfect example of that.

I've received a number of e-mails from women I don't know but who obviously know me. What they all have in common is a desire to either know me better or, in some cases, marry me. Some even send me pictures. One of Natasha, who describes herself as a Russian farm girl, is particularly fetching.

It's hard to understand. Natasha is obviously sensitive and caring; she tells me that she is lonely and her only goal is to please a man, in this case, me. You would think a woman like that wouldn't have to search for love on the Internet. It's flattering, but also sad, in a way.

"What are you doing?" Laurie asks, having come into the den behind me without my realizing it.

"Reading my fan mail. I've got quite the following in Russia."

"Natasha?" she asks.

"How did you know?"

"I got the same e-mail."

I give her my most lascivious grin. "Well,

that Natasha is really something."

"You should call her," she says. "I'm going to bed."

"Me, too," I say. It's an instinctive reaction; I would respond the same way if Laurie said that to me in court, during my closing argument.

"Aren't you researching the case?"

I nod. "Yes, but not getting anywhere. I'm just gathering information on how to acquire and administer botulinum toxin."

"I hope you never get charged with a crime," she says.

"Why do you say that?"

"Because they always go into the accused person's computer and find out he looked up stuff like 'how to strangle' and 'how to make a homemade hand grenade.' They'd find that you look up some very incriminating stuff."

"Fortunately they didn't find anything like that on Denise's computer," I say, and then a thought hits me. It's a rare feeling; these days I get hit by thoughts about as often as Muhammad Ali throws left hooks. I get up to look through the files.

"What are you looking for?" Laurie asks.

Before I answer, I quickly scan the table of contents to confirm that I'm right. "They looked through Denise's computer because they were trying to find evidence of guilt."

She nods. "Which they didn't find."

"Right, but they never did the same kind of examination of Barry's computer. They searched his e-mails, probably to see if there were threats from Denise, something like that. But they never searched the history."

"History of what?"

"Where he went online the last couple of weeks. I'm pretty sure you can do that. Sam once told me that every time you move around online, you leave a footprint."

"You do."

"So maybe if we get Barry's computer, we can find out what led him to Susser in the first place."

"Where is that computer now?"

"I'm sure the prosecutor has it. We didn't request it; I just never thought to use it to follow his cyber trail."

I call Hike and ask him to request the computer; then I call Sam to tell him to then get the computer from Hike and get to work on tracing Barry's steps.

Sam answers on the first ring, as he always does. I think he keeps his phone Krazy Glued to his ear. But this time he's whispering, and when I ask why, he says, "Crash is asleep."

"Sam, he sleeps all day."

"He's been through a lot, Andy. I hit him with my car."

"I remember," I say and then tell Sam about the computer and what I want him to do. I think he says it's a great idea, but it's really hard to hear him.

I hang up and ask Laurie if she thinks I should e-mail Natasha back and let her down gently.

"You do that," she says. "I'm still going to bed."

I close my computer. "The hell with Natasha," I say. "Commie bitch."

Everyone was in place, well ahead of schedule. In fact, had Carter realized it was going to go so smoothly and quickly, he might likely have delayed the beginning of the process.

The longer the men were in the field, the more chance there was for detection, for something to go wrong. They were well trained and had performed flawlessly to that point, but anything was possible.

Certainly Carter knew that his superior would never change the operation date. It was chosen for maximum psychological effectiveness, and Carter considered it a brilliant stroke. If 9/11 proved anything, and Carter believed it proved a great deal, it was that the American psyche was fragile.

Carter was a micromanager, and it had served him well to this point. He was earning a stunning amount of money for his role in this undertaking, but money was not what it was about for him. This was his chance to change the world for the better, and he was not about to see it achieve less than total success.

So he insisted on knowing everything that was happening at every moment, and the men in the field were instructed to communicate daily, even when there was nothing of consequence to report.

There was another reason for this documentation: Carter's superior had insisted on it. He believed that when the operation was concluded, when total success was achieved, it could become a template, or at least a helpful guide, to future operations, in countries around the world.

So for now the men were where they needed to be, doing nothing to attract undue attention. None knew any details about the operation in other cities, so in the unlikely event of exposure, the damage would be unwanted, but limited.

The target list had been chosen long ago, though it was somewhat arbitrary. It relied on knowing where each target would be on the day in question. In the event that the target changed his or her plan, it would not necessitate a change in the operation. The collateral damage alone would make it more than worthwhile.

But any such change in plans was unlikely. The chosen targets were people who loved the spotlight, who needed it to thrive. They wanted to show how genuinely and deeply they mourned those who had given their lives for their country.

Never mind the lives they had taken in the process.

No, these targets would be where they were supposed to be.

And soon Americans would have another reason to observe Memorial Day.

Jury selection is my second least favorite part of a trial. The only part I hate more is waiting for the verdict; that is the absolute worst.

Both of those times are tension filled, but in the case of the verdict, everyone involved in the trial, even those watching from the gallery, are aware of the importance of the moment.

Jury selection seems to everyone except the lawyers to be a tedious ritual, something to be gotten through before the real action can begin. Most people don't see it as having much drama.

But to me, and to the lawyers I am up against, it is a frustratingly crucial time. It's crucial because if the wrong person gets on the jury, the trial can be lost, or at least the possibility of winning can be pretty much eliminated, before it even begins.

The frustrating part is that, for all the reliance on sophisticated jury selection techniques, lawyers are mostly flying blind. That is because potential jurors are basically full of shit. They come in with an agenda, and during voir dire questioning their goal is to further that agenda.

They might lie to get on the jury or lie to get off it. Or they might have read everything about the crime, decided the defendant is guilty, and come in with the goal of sending him or her to prison. Of course they don't say that in court. Instead they say they know nothing about the case and vow to be open-minded.

That's not to say it's not tedious, because it is. The process of selecting Denise Price's jury is no different from every other one. We ask the questions, hear the answers, don't believe a thing they say, make our best guess, and hope.

Thomas Bader does a competent job questioning the candidates, but there aren't many lawyers who don't. What worries me about him is the way he carries himself. He's confident and relaxed, with an easy manner that will tend to ingratiate him with the twelve people we pick.

As the trial date has approached, Bader has gotten progressively less cooperative, as if he were putting his game face on. A good example of this was our request for Barry Price's computer. It seemed to take Bader by surprise, and he delayed turning it over to us.

My guess is that he was worried about why we were asking and realized that his people had not gone over the computer thoroughly enough. They probably took the time to do that before giving it to us.

Other than the annoying delay, that doesn't worry me much. They would be concerned with what is on the computer, e-mails, Web sites, etc. They would be less interested in where Barry had been in the weeks before his death, but even if they did look at that, it wouldn't have helped them much.

They wouldn't see the significance in financial searches Barry made online; they would just attribute that to normal business dealings. And they also would have no way of knowing that anything concerning Donald Susser would be meaningful to our case.

When Hike finally got the computer and gave it to Sam, his eyes lit up at the prospect of digging into it, since Barry seems to have been something of his computer idol. It's been three days since then and not a word from Sam.

We've seated eight of the twelve jurors so

far today, and as the session winds down, I'm feeling pretty good about it, or maybe pretty bad about it. I'm not really sure. The only thing I know for a fact is that the last juror to be questioned is someone Bader obviously wants, which means it's someone I therefore don't want.

The prospective juror's name is Doug Millman, and I don't like him. He's got a smug smile that silently claims to know it all, and I'm afraid that future fellow jurors might believe him. He's also a vice president at a midsize bank, and that background might make him sympathetic to Barry Price and therefore more likely to convict his accused killer.

Under Bader's questioning, Millman says that he knows absolutely nothing about the case, hasn't seen TV coverage, and hasn't read anything in the newspapers. He's obviously been living in a plastic bubble.

I'm not going to accept him on the jury, so I could just ask him a question or two and then send him on his way. But he gets on my nerves, so I take it a step further. In case you haven't already figured this out, I'm not the most mature guy in the room.

"Mr. Millman, did you vote in the recent election?"

He nods. "I did."

"First time?"

"No, I vote every time. Always have."

"Without telling us who you voted for, how did you make your decision?"

"What do you mean?"

"I mean, how did you learn about the candidates? Newspaper articles? TV? Did you see any of their speeches?"

He's already trapped, but he searches for a way out. "Mostly talking with friends."

"So, word of mouth?"

"Right."

"Your friends monitor the news, and then they tell you the facts so you can decide? Sort of like your own private researchers?"

"We just talk about what's going on in the world. My friends are smart people."

"But it's all one way, right? You're cut off from traditional sources of information, so you rely on them?"

"Mostly, but not completely. I'll read some about it also, just not the crime pages."

"Financial pages? Because of your job?"

Barry Price's murder was all over the financial pages, so Millman says, "I sometimes skim them."

"You wrote on your information sheet that you live alone. Do you have a television?"

"Yes."

"Cable?"

205

"Yes."

"Internet?"

"Yes."

"But you avoid the news at all costs in all of these media?"

"Mostly, as much as I can."

"Your smart friends, are some of them your coworkers? Friends in your industry?"

"Yes."

"So you work in the financial world, one of the leaders of that world is murdered, but your smart friends, the ones who keep you informed about current events, never even mentioned it?"

"Not that I remember."

"Mr. Millman, have your smart friends ever had occasion to tell you what 'perjury' means?"

"I know what it means."

"So if you were to get on this jury, and a lawyer, maybe someone like me, decided to have his investigators check out some of your statements today, you wouldn't worry?"

"No," he says, though he is obviously very worried. He keeps stealing glances at Bader, as if he's going to get help there. Bader, of course, knows by now that Millman is getting nowhere near the jury, so he just lets him twist in the wind.

"If investigators were to interview your smart friends, or perhaps subpoena your TV watching records, or your personal computer to check your Internet searches, you'd be fine?"

Millman is desperately trying to get out of this. "I don't remember seeing or hearing anything about Mr. Price's murder. It's possible that I did and I just forgot."

"Good-bye, Mr. Millman. You're excused."

I dread going through another day of this tomorrow, and to give myself a break, I change my plans for the evening. Rather than go home and plow through more of the case documents, I'm going to head to Charlie's to spend some time drinking beers and eating burgers with Vince and Pete.

It is a measure of how much I hate jury selection that I am viewing Vince as a more pleasant alternative.

But it doesn't matter, because as it turns out, I'm not going to Charlie's at all. As I approach my car, Sam calls on my cell phone. He sounds excited.

"Andy, I've got big news."

"Crash lost his first tooth? He barked 'dada'?"

"It's Barry's computer."

"What about it?"

"I hit the mother lode."

"He went to places I couldn't get near," Sam says. "I mean, I knew he was good, better than me, but I didn't see how he could be that good."

"What kind of places are we talking about?"

"Online. He was breaking into sites that I couldn't get into. That I doubted anyone could get into."

"How did he do it?" I ask.

"He got the passwords."

"How did he do that?"

"He had a password-crashing program with 25 AMD Radeon GPUs."

"I always wanted one of those," I say, "but my parents bought me a G.I. Joe instead."

"Let me explain," he says, and though I know I won't understand it, he seems so excited that I let him continue.

"Passwords are starting to become obsolete," he says.

"Really? I hardly use my computer, and I must have twenty passwords."

He nods. "Right, and they've got to be a certain number of characters, and some of them make you include cap letters and numbers and even symbols."

"Yup."

"Well, each letter, or whatever, is called a hash. So let's say your password has fifteen hashes, of all types, okay? This program can figure it out in less than ten minutes. And it doesn't have to know your dog's name or birthday or anything like that."

"How does it do it?"

"It bombards the target with combinations. This program can try a hundred billion hashes per second, and there are programs faster than that. Eventually it hits on the password, sooner rather than later."

"So it keeps getting them wrong until it gets them right?"

"Exactly," he says. "You should see how this thing works. Hilda and Morris are like kids in a candy store with it."

"I don't understand. If I type my password wrong twice on one of my sites, they lock the account and make me spend the next twelve hours on the phone with customer service telling them my mother's maiden name."

"But Barry wasn't breaking into individual accounts. He wasn't technically even breaking into the sites. He was breaking into the place where they store the passwords. Once he did that, he had free rein to go wherever he wanted."

"So where did he go?" I ask.

"We don't know yet. But we will."

"So if passwords are obsolete, what's going to replace them?"

"Nobody's figured that out yet."

I ask Sam to devote as much time as he can to tracing Barry Price's cyber steps, and he promises that he will. Then I head home to Laurie and Tara.

Any potential witnesses that I don't have time to interview I turn over to Laurie. Any competent person can get the information from them about what they're going to say and why they're going to say it. But Laurie has the ability to tell me more about each of them, to know what makes them tick, and to figure out their strengths and weaknesses.

Hike is a great lawyer, but when he interviews a witness, I ask him to give me a written report about it. That's because all I'm going to get from him are the facts; talking to Laurie supplies the nuance. And nuance in a cross-examination is everything.

I'm as ready for the trial as I can be, given the weapons at my disposal. Unfortunately, I wouldn't describe myself as heavily armed.

"Barry Price died in a plane that crashed, but he didn't die in a plane crash," is how Thomas Bader begins his opening argument to the jury. The final constitution of the jury is one I think I'm happy with; I'll know for sure a few seconds after the verdict is read.

"People die in plane crashes, fortunately not very often, but it happens. Barry Price was an experienced pilot, so he knew the risks as well as anyone. He knew that every time he went up, there was that danger, no matter how much care is taken."

Bader shakes his head sadly, as if he is reflecting thoughtfully on events, as if he hasn't rehearsed these words at least a dozen times. "But there was a danger he had not anticipated, one that had nothing to do with weather, or mechanical failure, or even pilot error. Because although Mr. Price's body was thrown seventy-five feet from the plane upon the terrible impact, the seeds of his death were planted well before that, in what he thought was the safety and comfort of his own home.

"The evidence will show that Barry Price was poisoned, and that is what caused his death. It was a poison that paralyzes before it kills, and there is every likelihood that he was alive, mentally alert, as he was forced to watch in terror as he lost control of his airplane.

"Yes, the airplane was a bit player in this tragedy. Barry Price died on a plane, but he would just as certainly have died in a car, or in a restaurant, or on a hammock, or maybe even in a hospital. The poison is that deadly.

"And that is why you are here, making the momentous decision you are going to make, rather than the National Transportation Safety Board. You are going to have to follow the evidence and decide who secretly administered the poison to Barry Price.

"And fortunately, the evidence is clear." Bader points to Denise. "This woman had the motive, the opportunity, and the means to have killed her husband. It was not the first time she had betrayed him, but it would be the last.

"The evidence will show, quite clearly, that Denise Price acquired the deadly toxin, slipped it into her husband's food or drink, and then coldly waited for him to die.

"It all made sense to her. It would give her freedom and huge sums of money with which to enjoy that freedom. And with his body burned beyond recognition in the crash, how would anyone ever know?

"Well, we do know, because things didn't quite work out as Denise Price had hoped. Her husband's body didn't burn in the crash. It was thrown from that crash and landed intact.

"And that simple fact enabled Barry Price, in death, to identify his murderer." He points at Denise again. "His wife, Denise Price.

"Thank you."

I have the option of delaying my opening statement until the beginning of the defense case, but it's an option I've never taken. By then the conviction boat could have sailed, and it's important that the jurors know now that there is another side to this story, one we will vigorously present.

It's also a good thing for Denise to hear someone advocate for her. She's just heard herself called a cold-blooded murderer by the State of New Jersey, which can have something of a chilling effect on one's mood.

I don't want her disconsolate; I want her

determined. That's for her sake but also, and more important, for the jurors, who can sense the difference.

"There are fifty-one people who could have murdered Barry Price," is how I begin, referring to those at the Price's party the night before his death. "And I'm only counting the ones who could have done it relatively easily. There are many others who could have done it as well, but it would have required a little more effort.

"The good news is that you don't have to figure out which of the fifty-one people committed this awful act. All you are being called on to do is conclude whether or not the prosecution has proved Denise Price guilty beyond a reasonable doubt.

"Now it is important for you to understand one thing going in: there is absolutely no direct evidence tying Denise Price to this crime. They'll tell you that she could have done it, they'll come up with reasons why they think she wanted to do it, and that's it. What they will present to you is not on the same planet as 'beyond a reasonable doubt.' "

I would love to be able to tell the jury about Donald Susser and the three murders in Augusta. But at this moment I have no hard evidence to connect them to Barry

Price, none at all, and Judge Hurdle would cut me off and admonish me in front of the jury. I can't afford to have the jury's first impression of our side be that we are trying to get away with something.

I don't point to Denise, as Bader did. Instead I walk over and place a hand on her shoulder. "Denise Price is a victim here. She has lost her husband, a man she loved for seventeen years, her high school sweetheart, her friend. You can't give back what she lost, but you can make sure that she doesn't lose any more.

"Look at the evidence and then do what is right. Give Denise Price her life back."

Denise looks somewhat relieved when I finish, and when I get back to the defense table she whispers a thank-you. She's had a rough time of it, but I will remind her that this is only the beginning. By the time Bader is finished presenting his case, she will look back on today with a nostalgic fondness.

Today will become one of the "good old days."

"He was my boss, my mentor, and most important, my friend."

That is how Mark Clemens responds when asked to describe his relationship with Barry Price. It is the first of many rehearsed lines that we will be hearing in Bader's direct examination of Clemens.

"What is the name of the company you work for?"

"The Price Group," Clemens says.

"Named for Barry Price? Bader asks. "He ran the firm?"

"He was the firm; he still is. We're following the strategies and guidelines he set."

"And your role there?"

"Executive vice president."

"So that is the number-two person in the firm?"

"Yes. But Barry was number one, and then there was everyone else."

Watching Clemens pretending to show

humility is like sticking my finger down my throat. But you learn the first day in law school that throwing up on the defense table is bad form, so I'm going to have to gag in silence.

Bader takes Clemens through the ownership of the firm. Clemens owns ten percent, three other executives own five percent each, and Price owned seventy-five percent. He willingly gives out the information that Denise Price would inherit Barry's ownership position.

Bader asks him some more questions about the business relationship and then moves to the personal. "How well do you know Denise Price?"

"I guess not as well as I thought," he says, and though Hurdle sustains my objection, the damage is done. He goes on to say that he always "liked" Denise, and the past tense conveys his meaning.

Bader asks how Clemens viewed the Prices' marriage.

"I didn't know them for the first seven years, and Barry told me that there was a time when it was wonderful, when they were very happy. Unfortunately, that didn't last."

He goes on to describe a loveless marriage, claiming that it was Barry's point of view. He says that Barry believed Denise was having an affair but could never prove it. "He was planning to leave her," Clemens says.

"When did he tell you that?"

"Three weeks before his death."

Bader then takes him to the party that Barry and Denise threw the night before his death and asks him about the argument they had.

"I was embarrassed for Barry," Clemens says. "But Denise was giving him a hard time, and I guess he couldn't just stand there and take it anymore. So he yelled at her, and that seemed to quiet her down. She had a lot to drink."

Bader spends some more time letting Clemens recount the horror that was Denise Price, and then he turns him over to me for cross-examination.

"Mr. Clemens, would you say that Barry Price felt his marriage had reached a point of no return?"

"Yes."

"How long had he felt that?"

"For a long time, at least a year or a year and a half. It had been deteriorating for much longer than that. But Barry wasn't a quitter; he kept trying to make it work."

"Until three weeks before, when he told you he was leaving? Or maybe longer?"

"It was three weeks."

"Is it possible he decided more than three weeks before but waited to tell you? Or did he tell you every personal thing the moment it entered his mind?"

I can see a flash of annoyance in Clemens's eyes, which is what I'm hoping for. "We were close, but I suppose it's possible it was longer than three weeks."

"So at least three weeks before his death, or maybe longer, he had decided to leave the marriage. Why do you think he didn't then do so right away?"

"There are plans one has to make," Clemens says.

"What kind of plans? There were no children to tell, were there?"

He shakes his head. "No."

"Did he need a place to stay, or did he have an apartment in New York City?"

"He did have an apartment. But there are financial arrangements to be made in a situation like that."

"Like protecting assets?"

"Yes."

"What moves did he make to do so in those three weeks?"

He hesitates, trying to decide how to put it. "I don't know."

"He never discussed it with you, his business partner and close friend? He told you intimate details about his personal life but not about his finances? As close as you were?"

"I'm not aware of any financial moves he made."

I drop that and take him back to the night of the party and again ask him about the argument that Barry and Denise had. "They were angry at each other? They raised their voices?"

"Yes."

I submit as evidence an article about Barry Price that ran in *Barron's* two years ago. It was basically a favorable piece, but it also described Barry as being known for his no-holds-barred business style, which resulted in his having a number of enemies in the industry.

"According to this article," I say, "Barry Price had a quick temper, which resulted in many loud arguments."

"It was his style," Clemens says. "But Barry would give anyone the shirt off his back."

"But it's fair to say he had business enemies, people who disliked or resented him?"

"Everyone does."

"Some of these people he raised his voice

to, and they raised their voices in return?"

"Yes, on occasion."

"To your knowledge, have any of them been charged with his murder?"

Bader objects and Hurdle sustains. My style is to jump around a lot; I found it throws adversarial witnesses off balance.

"Do you know where Barry Price was flying to the night he died?"

"Augusta, Maine."

"He told you that?"

"No, Mr. Bader mentioned it."

I smile. "Did Mr. Bader discuss a lot of the evidence with you?"

"No."

"Do you know why Barry Price was flying to Maine?"

"No, I don't."

"He never told you that either?"

"No."

I drop that, though it will help me later in the trial. I then introduce as evidence a floor plan of the Price house and ask where the argument took place. He points to the living room area.

"So you were there at the time, right? You spent most of your time that night in that room?"

He nods. "Yes."

"Is that where the buffet was as well?"

"Yes."

"And the music?"

"Yes?"

"So that was the center of the party, where most of the people stayed?"

"Yes."

I point to the diagram. "So there was no way you could see this door, the one to the basement, correct?" In the basement is where they found traces of the poison in the sink.

He knows where I'm going, but there's nothing he can do about it now. "Not from where I was, no."

"So any of the fifty-one people at the party could have gone into that basement, and neither you nor anyone else in that room would know it, correct?"

"Yes."

"Thank you, Mr. Clemens, you've been very helpful."

"Imachu. It's a Turkish company, banking out of Belize," Sam says.

I have absolutely no idea why a Turkish company would be banking in Belize, unless maybe they waive their ATM fees there. But Sam seems really excited about what he's found, so I'm not going to interrupt him.

"They have eight hundred and thirty million dollars in Barry's company, which makes them the second biggest investor."

"What does the company do?" I ask.

"I haven't a clue. There's no evidence that they do anything other than invest money. But it could be that I'm just not finding it; maybe they have subsidiaries that make widgets."

"What did you find out about them?"

Sam smiles, preparing to relish his triumph. "Well, I was over in the bunker last night, the team had gone home, and . . ."

"You go to the bunker even when the group is not there?"

"Sure, we have a whole computer setup there. Anyway, I was sitting at the computer and talking to Crash —"

"You bring Crash to the Holiday Inn?"

"Of course. The desk clerk loves him."

"Sam . . ."

"Anyway, I said to Crash, 'This company takes in a lot of money from their investments. Barry alone has gotten them almost twelve percent this year.' "

"Did Crash think that was high?"

"I don't know, but it got me to thinking. Where is that money going? So I found out." He pauses for effect. "One of the places their money went was to a bank account in the Caymans, but it didn't stay there for long."

This is potentially such interesting news that I'm not even going to make another snide Crash crack, although I have a good one ready. "Keep talking," I say.

"They sent out a bunch of wires from their Cayman account." Another smile. "And one of them went to none other than Donald Susser, who then divvied it up among his friends."

"This is terrific, Sam. Great work."

"You might want to hold the praise until I

226

get to the good part. Another wire went to a guy named Alex Larsen, in Concord, New Hampshire."

"The name is familiar," I say. "Who is he?"

"Who was he," Sam corrects. "He was one of four people gunned down in a garage a while back. An undercover cop was one of the people killed."

"I remember reading about it. So Barry invests money for this company, they send some of it to people in New England, who then wind up dead."

"They sent other wires out as well, one of them went to a guy in Columbus, Ohio, but I haven't tracked them all down yet," Sam says. "I figured you'd want to know about this right away."

"Thanks, Sam, you did the right thing. Now take Crash, and the two of you find out where the other wires went."

"Will do. I'm just going to stop at the prison first, if that's okay."

"What for?"

"I've been visiting Denise on and off. She feels really alone."

I'm not sure I think Sam is in a good place on this. From what I know about our case, he's not likely to be taking Denise to the prom any time soon. "Okay, but . . . be careful with this."

"It's under control."

When Sam leaves, I head home to discuss this development with Laurie. I'm in the middle of a trial, so there is no time to lose in finding out how all this fits into the puzzle that is Barry Price's death.

"Contacting the Concord police won't get you much," Laurie says, and as a former police chief she is in a good position to make that assessment. "They're not going to tell you details of their investigation, and I doubt very much that they know anything that ties it to Susser and Augusta."

"I could ask Pete to do it for me."

She nods, or maybe it's a shrug. "And he'd probably do it."

"But it would be too little, too late," I say. "Local Concord cops probably have no idea of the big picture."

Her nod is more vigorous this time. "Andy, this is federal. At the very least it's a conspiracy to murder across state lines. There is no way to know how far this goes, but what we know by itself is enough. I think your first call should be to Cindy."

This is unprecedented. Cindy Spodek is a friend of Laurie's and mine who also happens to be the second in command at the FBI's Boston office. I call upon her for help far more than I should, and way more than

Laurie thinks I should. If Laurie is making the suggestion, she must think it's very important to take this route.

I call her office, and Cindy gets on the phone. "Let me venture a wild guess, Andy. You have a client, and you need my help."

"How wrong you are," I say. "Laurie and I are coming to Boston, and we're hoping to take you and Tom to dinner."

"Thank you. I'll bring Robert."

"The more the merrier."

"My husband's name is Robert, not Tom."

Cindy got married a few years back, but I was in trial and we didn't go to the wedding. I've actually never met Robert, or whatever the hell his name is.

"That Robert is one lucky man, and Tom really missed the boat."

"When are you coming to Boston?"

"Not sure yet," I say. "At some point."

"Great, I think we're free then. I'll make a reservation. Seafood okay?"

"Sounds great."

"What do you want, Andy?"

"Hold on," I say and hand the phone to Laurie. "This isn't going well."

Laurie gets on, and after a few minutes of chitchat tells Cindy that she suggested I call, that the subject matter is very important. Cindy knows that Laurie, unlike me, would never bullshit her, so when I get back on the phone her attitude has changed.

I lay out for her what I know about Susser and the murders in Augusta, and how they tie in, at least financially, with the deaths in New Hampshire. Just to make sure, I use the magic word: "assassinations."

Cindy listens and asks only a few questions. When we're finished, she says, "I'll get back to you."

Which she will.

I have to pick and choose my spots. It's a fine line. I don't want to overdo my attacking of prosecution witnesses, particularly when they are all saying basically the same thing. It could look like I'm being overly argumentative in an attempt to prevent the jury from learning the truth.

A good example is the string of witnesses Bader brings in to say that Barry and Denise Price's marriage was in major trouble. Clemens had said the same thing, and there is no doubt that it is true.

Confronting each of the witnesses in an attempt to try and disprove what they are saying would be futile. That is especially true since what they are saying is not that terribly incriminating; marriages go bad all the time without murder being the result. My former wife and I wound up getting divorced, but we didn't toast the occasion with a botulism cocktail.

So I've been biding my time, asking questions to show that I'm awake and alert and that our side has a point of view. But I don't go so far as to vigorously dispute obvious truths, especially when they're not all that damaging in the first place.

But Cynthia Walling is different. Bader's other witnesses, like Clemens, have been Barry's friends and associates, so they have been presenting things from what they claim was his point of view. Walling was a friend of Denise's, so her words will have more impact.

"She was having an affair," says Walling, "and she thought he was as well. She wanted out of the marriage."

I knew from the discovery documents that she was going to say this, but hearing it in court seems to magnify its impact. The jurors look like they're hanging on every word.

"Why didn't she just file for divorce?" asks Bader.

"She was afraid that Barry would take all their money and leave her with nothing."

"And money is important to Denise?"

"Very."

Denise seems to be having trouble maintaining the dispassionate look I counseled that she keep. She doesn't take her eyes off the woman she thought was her friend, and it is clear that she is angry.

But Walling doesn't back off, and the testimony itself only gets worse. Walling paints a thoroughly unflattering picture of Denise, culminating in her recounting of a conversation in which she says Denise wished "Barry would die."

I discussed Walling's upcoming testimony with Denise a while back. She denied that she was having an affair or saying that she wanted out of the marriage or that she hoped something bad would happen to Barry. Her explanation for why Walling would say these kinds of things was jealousy and a belief that Walling had always had a "thing" for Barry.

I can't be sure that Denise was telling me the truth. In fact I wouldn't be surprised if she was not. She might well have been having an affair, but that is a long way from murder. In any event, I have to act on the assumption that Denise is being straight with me. And if that is the case, then Walling is lying.

"Ms. Walling, you and Denise were close friends?"

"Very."

"You shared things, had a very open, intimate relationship?"

"Yes. We would have long conversations like that."

"Who was she having an affair with?"

"I don't know."

"She didn't tell you?"

"No," she says. "I think she was protecting the man."

"Telling you would be endangering him?"

"Maybe that's what she thought."

"Where did they meet?" I ask.

"I don't know."

"How often did they meet?"

"I'm not sure."

"Did she say who she thought Barry was having an affair with?"

"No."

"How did she know he was?"

"I'm not sure."

"Maybe your intimate conversations with Denise weren't as long as you remembered," I say. Bader objects, and Judge Hurdle admonishes me for my sarcasm.

"You say that Denise told you she wished Barry were dead."

"Yes."

"When was that?"

"Probably about six weeks before he died."

"Did you view that as a threat?"

"I was worried about it."

"You thought she might do something to

hasten his death?"

"I thought something was possible, that's all."

"You mean you thought she might murder him?"

"I wouldn't say I thought that. I just thought it was possible. Denise was very angry and very upset."

"Did you call the police?"

"No."

"Did she ever mention it again?"

"No."

"How many conversations did you have with her after the one in which she said she wished he was dead?"

She thinks for a moment. "Maybe ten."

"So, just so I understand, you had ten more intimate, open conversations with someone you thought might possibly commit a murder? What does somebody have to say to get you to be less open and intimate?"

"I just wasn't ready to believe it could happen," Walling says.

"When was the last time you spoke with Denise Price?"

"At her house after Barry's memorial service."

"So you thought Denise might possibly murder her husband, then soon afterward he died a violent death, and you still stood by her?" I ask, not having to try hard to sound incredulous.

"We thought it was a plane crash then. No one knew he was murdered. I read that it was a possibility in the paper the next day."

"And then you went to the police and said, 'I think Denise might have done it'?"

"No. I . . ."

"Do you have a phone? E-mail? Do you live near a mailbox? Did you have no way to turn in someone you thought was a murderer?"

Bader jumps out of his chair to object, but Hurdle sustains it before he gets a chance. Hurdle warns me about my behavior, which seems to surprise him.

He obviously never checked me out.

"Ms. Walling, you were close friends with Denise Price. What did you like about her? I mean before this all happened."

She's not sure how to answer this; she's come to bury Denise, not to praise her. "Well, she's very smart. And she was independent, she was her own person."

I nod. "Worldly? Knew how to handle herself?"

"Yes."

"Smart, worldly, independent . . . does that sound like the kind of person who would let her husband take the money and run? Or does that sound like the kind of person who would call a good lawyer and make sure she got what the law said she should get?"

Before Walling can answer, I continue. "Why would a smart person risk a life in prison to get money that she could get just by picking up the phone?"

Bader objects that it's outside the scope of the witness's direct testimony and knowledge, and Hurdle agrees.

Walling would not have been able to answer that question, and I'm hoping that the jury can't either.

Judge Hurdle has given us today off, citing "calendar issues." I'm hoping those issues will last a really long time, because every day we get closer to a verdict is another day we're in ever-increasing trouble.

This morning I'm at the Tara Foundation, a responsibility I have completely neglected since the trial began. It's characteristic of Willie and Sondra that they don't make me feel guilty, pointing out that this is their job and they love it.

It must be nice to be able to say that.

I play with the dogs for about an hour and then go into the office to do some of the legal and tax work for the foundation that I've fallen behind on. Willie stays with the dogs, while Sondra is in the office with me, fielding phone calls from potential adopters.

I'm there for only about five minutes when the door opens and two men come in. Based on their look and the way they are dressed, there is approximately a hundred and fifty percent chance that they are federal agents. Of course, that could be a conservative estimate.

"I'm Special Agent Muñoz," one of them says, as he shows me his ID. "This is Special Agent Shales."

Something about his tone annoys me, but then again, I get annoyed really easily. "Gee," I say, "I think all you agents are pretty special."

"Your wiseass reputation is apparently well deserved," Muñoz says, which means he's spoken to Cindy Spodek.

I look past them to the door, where Willie is coming toward us. He's moving quickly and quietly, which leads me to believe he might think these guys are here to do me harm.

"Willie!" I yell. "There are two FBI agents I'd like you to meet. Guys, this is my partner, Willie Miller, and this is his wife, Sondra. Willie, these are two very special agents."

Willie stops short, lending credibility to my fear that he was coming in to protect me. Willie can do a lot of damage in a very short amount of time.

"Can we speak somewhere alone?" Muñoz asks.

"I trust these people with my life, Senator. If I ask them to leave, it would be an insult." I'm doing Michael Corleone from *The Godfather*, but this irritating attitude I'm exhibiting is not an effort to be obnoxious, even though I'm succeeding at it.

I've done a lot of business with the FBI, and it's always a power struggle. I'm going to want information from them, and they're certainly going to want some from me, so I need to show them I'm not in the least bit intimidated.

Sondra, who has seen me be obnoxious on all kinds of occasions, says, "Come on, Willie. Let's let them talk."

Willie looks at me, and I give him a short nod confirming that it's okay. He and Sondra leave, and Muñoz says, "Tell us about Augusta."

"Tell me about Concord, New Hampshire."

"Exactly what kind of game are you playing, Carpenter? You're a smart guy; you know we can make things difficult for you."

"If you spoke to Cindy Spodek about me, then you know what I'm about to say, but I'll say it anyway. I'm defending my client. That is my first and last responsibility. If in

240

the process of doing that I can help the cause of truth and justice, I'm happy to do it. But if you'd rather try and make things difficult for me, take your best shot. But first get the hell out of here."

This seems to have its desired effect, and the horse trading begins. I agree to tell them what I know about Susser and Augusta, and they agree to do the same about Concord. Each of us knows that the other will be withholding something, but at least it's a start.

Ever cooperative, I agree to go first, and I describe how we connected Barry to Susser through his phone records, supplemented by the knowledge that Barry was flying to Augusta when he died. I tell them how my supposedly private meeting with Susser expanded and how they told us about Carter and the assassination for hire, without their revealing who the target was.

"Why would they tell you all that?" Agent Shales asks, the first time he has spoken since they got here.

"I brought along a friend who is the type people just seem to open up to."

"So how did you connect all this to what happened in Concord?"

"Concord? Doesn't ring a bell."

They understand that it's their turn, and

Muñoz does the talking. He tells me about an undercover cop named Drew Keller, who got killed investigating what he believed might be an assassination plot. The guys he was dealing with also got killed, and since then they have been unsuccessful in identifying either the killer or the planned assassination target.

With that out of the way, the real negotiation can begin. "Okay, I'll tell you what the connection between the two is. I won't tell you how I made that connection, nor is it important."

"Good," Muñoz says, acting as if the deal has been sealed. He knows better, but he's playing the game.

"That's the quid," I say. "Here comes the pro quo. There is no doubt in my mind that Barry Price was not murdered by his wife over an affair or alimony. His murder has to be tied up in whatever is behind all these other killings."

Muñoz nods. "Seems like a fair bet."

"But nothing that we've talked about is admissible at trial, at least not at this point. So as you learn things, particularly things that are relevant to my client's case, I expect to be informed of them."

Muñoz nods. "As best I can."

I know what he means. There are things

he might not be able to reveal; some could even be classified.

"And if there are things you learn, significant information that could get my client off, you'll testify at trial. If there are other ways for me to get the information in, I'll do so. But if not, you take the stand."

Muñoz thinks about it for a moment; this is a big ask. Finally he nods. "You have my word."

I don't know him, so I have no idea whether he is telling the truth. I'll ask Cindy whether I can rely on him, but for now, I have no choice.

"There's a company named Imachu. It's a Turkish company that does banking in Belize and the Caymans and who knows where else. Barry Price's company invests a lot of their money."

Unless these guys are great actors, their expressions tell me they've never heard of the company. I continue, "They wired a lot of money to Donald Susser, and they also wired it to one of the dead guys in Concord."

"How did you trace that money?" Muñoz asks. They must have tried and run into a brick wall. Sam told me Barry's password machine can get them places the U.S. government can't go to. Of course Sam doesn't have to worry about such things as international banking regulations or privacy laws or search warrants.

The bottom line is that the federal government is a step behind Hilda and Eli Mandlebaum.

"That I can't share with you. But the information is solid."

"Is there anyone else who has received money from that company that we should know about?"

"I'm finding that out now. If there is, I'll let you know."

We talk a little more, but it's only so each side can see if there's any more advantage to be gained. Before they leave, Muñoz reminds me to give him any additional names that have received wired money from the same account as Susser and the guy in Concord. I renew my promise that I will.

"See you around," Muñoz says as they leave.

I give him my sweetest smile. "That'll give me something to look forward to."

As soon as they leave, I call Sam and ask if he's found other recipients of the money yet.

"There's a guy in Ohio I told you about; we're still in the process of checking him out. There are a couple others also. We're close, Andy, but it's slow going."

"E-mail me the information as you get it. I need to turn it over to the FBI."

"The FBI's in this now?"

"Yes."

"On our side?"

"Of course. Don't we represent truth, justice, and the American way?"

Christopher Schroeder is an expert on poisons. Actually, he looks like he's been sucking some down for a while. He's at least six two but can't weigh more than a hundred and fifty pounds, and he isn't just pale, he is entirely without skin color.

Schroeder is a sixty-four-year-old professor of chemistry at Columbia University, but at this stage of his career, he spends more time testifying than he does professing.

He learned a number of years ago that there is more money to be made showing off knowledge in front of a jury than in front of undergraduates. Other than the financial remuneration, there's not much difference for him: both jurors and students have to fight to stay awake when he talks.

Bader no doubt recognizes that Schroeder is dull as dirt, so he tries to move the testimony along at a rapid pace. He quickly has Schroeder relate his credentials, which are impressive and certainly establish him as an expert in the field.

The subject of today's class is botulinum poisoning, and Schroeder quite literally wrote the book on it. He's written a textbook on poisonous substances, which I glanced at last night. It's not exactly a laugh riot, but it suits Schroeder's personality perfectly.

Schroeder says that the botulinum toxin is relatively easy to acquire, and that all one has to do is spend minutes online to learn how.

Bader can't be thrilled with that comment, since part of the rationale for his case is Denise's pharmaceutical background. "So someone with Denise Price's experience could do so relatively easily?" he asks.

"No question about it."

They then move on to the delayed reaction of the poison, which is especially crucial. No one contends that a killer was on the plane with Barry, so when and how it was administered is something Bader needs to deal with.

Schroeder says that it takes anywhere from six to twenty-four hours for symptoms to appear, but once they do, incapacitation is rapid. The timing of the symptoms, according to Schroeder, can be adjusted by someone knowledgeable, based on the amount of the poison and the way it is administered. This, Bader has him point out, is where Denise's expertise would be especially valuable.

"The impact is mostly muscular," Schroeder says. "Starts with the facial muscles; the eyelids will droop, and the subject will have difficulty swallowing and chewing. Then it spreads downward, at a pace depending on the severity. It will reach the respiratory system, making breathing progressively more difficult and eventually impossible, and paralysis will set in."

Schroeder says that Barry would likely have been mentally alert but unable to physically do anything to stop the plane's descent. It is a nightmare situation, and the jury actually physically recoils from the horror of it.

Schroeder is a thoroughly credible witness, which happens to be the type I hate most. I should let Hike cross-examine him, since he considers himself an expert on poison. But having to watch and listen to a conversation between two people that depressing could cause mass suicide in the gallery.

Judge Hurdle gives everyone a fifteen-minute break before I question Schroeder. I use the time to check my phone, and I see that Sam had e-mailed me the information that someone named Kyle Austin of Columbus, Ohio, had received one hundred thousand from Imachu in the same manner as Susser and the others.

I quickly call Muñoz and tell him about Austin and then head back into the courtroom.

"Professor Schroeder, about how many cases of botulism are there each year? If you know . . ."

He flashes a glare at my raising the possibility that there is something about this subject he might not know. "There are slightly more than a hundred cases on average in the United States each year, just under a thousand worldwide."

"And what percentage of those are classified as murders?" I ask.

"I don't have that statistic, but it would be very low. The botulinum toxin occurs naturally."

"So for all the testifying you've done, it's never been in a criminal case?"

"No, always civil. They generally concern whether negligence caused the poisoning."

I've put in the jurors' minds that perhaps this isn't even a murder, but it's only a temporary victory, since later evidence will definitely establish it as a murder. Having said that, the muddier the water, the better I like it.

"Now, you talked about the wide variance of time it can take for the poison to kick in."

He smiles without humor. "I don't believe I used the words 'kick in.' "

I smile back. "Do you want me to translate?"

He shakes his head. "Not necessary."

"Then you said that the time between ingestion and symptoms can be controlled, based on the amount administered and the form it was in."

He nods. "Correct."

I introduce a book as evidence, point to a sentence, and ask Schroeder to read it aloud for the jury.

Before he does so, he says, "I see what you're getting at, but —"

I interrupt him. "Please just read the sentence . . . that way we can let the jurors in on it."

He starts to argue again, but this time Judge Hurdle steps in and instructs him to read.

" 'The incubation period after ingestion is decidedly unpredictable.' "

"Thank you. So we now have something of a dilemma here. You've said in court that it can be predictable, and the author of that text said it is 'decidedly unpredictable.' It's a regular battle of the experts. By the way, who wrote that book?"

"I did," says Schroeder, through teeth that seem somewhat clenched. "But I was referring to an accidental situation where the amount and manner of ingestion were not known."

"Oh, sorry. Can you read from the paragraph where you say that?"

"It's not included in the book."

"Did you write a sequel to this book, where you clear up mistakes like that?"

Schroeder is unable to conceal his annoyance. "It was not a mistake."

"Fine. Let's leave it there. The sentence you read was not a mistake. Glad we cleared that up."

Bader objects, but Hurdle overrules him, which qualifies as a news event.

"Professor, if Barry Price was murdered, who did it?"

"What do you mean?"

"Which part didn't you understand? If someone intentionally gave him the poison, who was it?"

"I couldn't say."

"Because you don't want to say or because you don't know?"

"I don't know."

"Join the club. Thank you."

You can't tell a bank by its lobby. The Island Bank of the Caribbean has a New York office on Madison Avenue and Forty-sixth Street, but if the name wasn't on the door, you'd never know it. It is all cold marble, and except for the faint strains of Caribbean music in the background, it's like every other bank in New York.

I take the elevator up to the fourth floor, and during the ride the music is louder. Even so, I don't think too many visitors to this place get the urge to take off their shoes and let the sand run through their toes.

I'm here to see Richard Glennon, a bank officer whom Sam discovered through his online shenanigans has been the person in charge of the Imachu account since his arrival at the company six months previous. Since Imachu wired the money to the now-deceased individuals in Augusta and Concord through Glennon's department, he may have relevant information to provide.

He expressed a reluctant willingness to talk to me but made sure I understood that we would talk only about generic issues, not the confidential specifics of the bank's client. That is certainly in line with my expectations, which are quite low. Basically I'm here because I have to be someplace, so this place is as good as any.

When I introduce myself at the reception desk, I discover that my meeting with Mr. Glennon has been preempted, and I'm instead meeting with Randall Franklin, the head of the area of the bank responsible for the department in which Glennon toils. I guess it makes sense, since I am the unquestioned head of the Andy Carpenter law firm.

We will be two titans of business, going one on one.

Franklin very much looks the part of the high-level successful banker, right down to the perfectly tailored, expensive suit, the dignified but smug manner, and the cleft in the chin on his good-looking face. Think Cary Grant without the charm.

"Due to the nature of your visit, I felt it more appropriate that you speak with me rather than Mr. Glennon, especially since he's relatively new here."

"I didn't even realize that my visit had a

nature," I say. "I certainly never mentioned it to anyone."

He smiles. "Intensive research was not required to figure it out. So what can I do for you?"

"You have a client named Imachu, a Turkish company."

The smile doesn't leave his face, and no words leave his mouth.

"That company has sent some wire transfers from your bank, which is what I'm interested in."

"Mr. Carpenter, you're a lawyer and no doubt well versed in matters of this kind. Surely you are aware that we would not be able to discuss any of our customer accounts with you. So I will neither confirm nor deny that this company you mention even banks here."

I nod. "So let's try it another way. Let's say any company has an account with your bank and they want to send a wire. Who on the company end would be empowered to authorize it?"

"There's no standard answer for that. It would be whoever the company so designates."

"And they could do it with a phone call?"

"Up to a preset amount; above that would require documentation."

"Does the bank do any check whatsoever on the recipients of the transfers?"

"Only in the rarest of cases; that is not our responsibility."

"What are the rarest of cases?" I ask. "Are there terrorist groups that you won't send money to?"

"Of course, providing the country we are operating in has placed restrictions in effect."

"Speaking of countries, why would an entity in another country use your bank?"

"You would have to ask them. But I assume it is because we provide professional service and ample opportunity for growth and investment." Another smile. "And we are discreet."

"Really?" I ask. "I hadn't noticed."

"Is there anything else I can help you with?"

"You can help me understand why you are letting a client use your bank to send money to murderers."

His expression doesn't change. "When and if you can provide proof of those allegations, we will take them very seriously."

I smile. "When I have proof, you'll have no choice."

Unless prompted into urgent action, bureaucracies can be ponderous. The FBI is no exception to this, but in tracking down Kyle Austin, they moved relatively quickly.

It wasn't urgent enough for Muñoz to go to Columbus himself, and in any event, he first wanted to do some background work on Austin. So he put in the request and asked for information ASAP.

An agent got to work on it within a couple of hours, and an hour after that he electronically reported back to Muñoz. Austin was an Iraqi vet, but he'd had some issues since his discharge.

He was convicted on a domestic violence charge, and though his girlfriend subsequently refused to testify, he did some jail time. He was out of work but had made some recent fairly expensive purchases, and three weeks prior had rented a house in an area that was an obvious step up from his previous residence.

Agent Jim Matuszak, working out of the Columbus office, was assigned to the case, and he and Muñoz connected on the phone at six that same evening. Muñoz updated him on where things stood, focusing on Austin's possible connection to it.

It was decided that Matuszak and another agent would bring Austin in for questioning the next morning. Muñoz would watch the interview on video but would not participate in it. If Austin seemed like a promising lead as it related to the case, then Muñoz would likely fly out to Columbus that afternoon for further questioning and investigation.

Of course, both men recognized the possibility that Austin would refuse to answer any questions or demand a lawyer before doing so. In that eventuality, it would kick Muñoz and the Bureau into a full-court press. Austin's life would be turned upside down in an effort to find out what he was hiding.

Matuszak and Agent Wilson Cardiff drove out to Austin's house at 8:00 A.M. as planned, but their arrival was delayed by the presence of police cars blocking off the street.

The agents presented their identification to Detective Lieutenant Nancy Francis of the Columbus PD, in charge at the scene, and asked what was going on.

"A woman named Lois Cassidy works as a cocktail waitress in town. She got off at two A.M. and came to this house, to see her boyfriend."

"Kyle Austin?" asked Matuszak.

Francis nodded. "Kyle Austin. He wasn't home, and she figured he was out, probably cheating on her. It apparently wouldn't have been the first time. But she couldn't reach him on the phone, so she went to sleep. In the morning, she decided to leave and noticed the garage door was open."

Matuszak took a quick look in the direction of the garage, which was where most of the people were. He assumed, correctly, that the forensics people were doing their work.

Francis continued. "His body was on the floor, one bullet in the back of the head at close range. Looks like he got hit just after he came home, coroner estimates some time between nine and midnight. Shooter was obviously a pro."

"Suspects?"

"Not yet," Francis said. "What's your interest in this?"

Matuszak was not about to share that with a local cop, at least not at that point. "We were hoping to question him."

"Good luck with that."

Today is the key day in the trial, at least so far. To the gallery, and the media that are covering it, it's going to seem dull and dry as dirt. Today we're going to discuss the forensic analysis of the traces of botulinum toxin. Oh, boy.

I arrive at court at eight thirty, as I do every day. On the way I call Sam to receive any updates he might have for me. Sam works late into the night, so the morning is usually a good time to speak to him.

Sam doesn't answer the phone, which is rather unusual. He and Crash are probably taking a bath. I make a note to call him during the first break this morning.

I take my seat at the defense table, where Hike is already waiting. Bader's team is at the prosecution table, but Bader hasn't arrived yet.

Almost the moment I sit down, the bailiff comes over to me and says, "Judge Hurdle wants to see you in chambers."

There's no sense asking why, since the bailiff would likely not know and certainly wouldn't tell me if he did. "Let's go," I say to Hike, but the bailiff shakes his head.

"The judge only wants to see you."

I've got an uneasy feeling about this, though there's not necessarily any reason to think it's anything of consequence. Most likely it's a juror issue; maybe one was acting improperly.

If that's the case, I hope "improperly" is understating the case, since a mistrial would be a gift from heaven. My first choice would be that the juror was caught in a sex romp with Bader, the judge, two other jurors, and the arresting officer. And to finish off my sure mistrial scenario, at the height of passion I hope the judge screamed, "The hell with fair trials!"

When I get to the judge's chambers, Bader is already there, alone with the judge. I'm not thrilled with this; proper procedure calls for the judge never to be with only one of the lawyers. But they don't seem to be talking, so it's likely a no-harm-no-foul situation.

"Mr. Carpenter, take a seat," Judge Hurdle says.

I do so and then ask, "What's going on?"

"I'm waiting for a phone call, and then we can begin. Should be just a few moments."

The few moments become ten of the most uncomfortable minutes I've ever experienced. Not a word is spoken, even if you're one of those people who consider eye contact to be speech.

Finally the ringing of the phone pierces the silence. The judge picks it up and says, "Yes?" then listens for maybe ten seconds. He follows that with "Thank you." Hurdle is one great conversationalist.

"Mr. Carpenter," he says, "I should start by informing you that Mr. Bader is already aware of what I'm about to say. He learned it here, in my chambers, minutes before your arrival."

I don't like the sound of this at all.

"Your client, Denise Price, asked to speak with me in private, and she did so last evening."

"Why wasn't I contacted?" I ask, now annoyed.

"Because she specifically asked that you not be," he says. "She had an agenda to discuss, and part of that agenda was to file a complaint about your actions in this case."

"What does that mean?"

"She said that you were aware that she possessed information that might have been exculpatory in nature, and that you insisted she not reveal it."

"This isn't making any sense." It's not often that I am completely bewildered, but that's what I am at the moment.

"I'm not commenting on the veracity of her statements, I'm merely summarizing them."

"What is the information she claims to have?" No matter where this goes from here, it is an unmitigated disaster.

"Let me continue," he says, as if I were stopping him. "She has admitted to an extramarital affair, and she believes that the man she was involved with murdered her husband."

"Who is that?" I ask, feeling like my head is about to explode.

"Samuel Willis. The police executed a search warrant on his home early this morning, and I was just advised in that telephone call that he has been placed under arrest."

Kaboom.

The judge goes on to tell me that he has no choice but to declare a mistrial. Denise is going to remain in custody. Far more investigation will be necessary before consideration could be given to dropping the charges against her.

He also says that he is obligated to commence an investigation into my conduct and whether or not Denise's charges have any merit. She has told him that she does not want to speak with me, and he directs me not to try. It's just as well, since I would probably strangle her.

But at this point I really don't care what he's saying. All I care about is finding Sam, wherever he has been taken.

He's going to need a lawyer.

Me.

Sam has been taken to the Passaic County Jail. That is because the arrest was made in Paterson, but once jurisdictional issues have been resolved, I'm quite sure he'll be transferred to Morris County.

I call Laurie on the way, and she is as stunned as I was. There will be time later for us to try and figure out what happened and why, and to talk strategy, but right now the only thing to do is help Sam.

Laurie does have one piece of information for me, though, which in its own way is another bombshell. Agent Muñoz called, asking to speak to me right away. She explained that she was my investigator and pressed him for information, so that she could determine whether it was important enough to interrupt me during the court day.

It would have been, that is, if I had a court day. Muñoz said that Kyle Austin, the

Columbus, Ohio, individual who had also received wired money, was murdered last night.

It is very significant news. I had basically been interested in Muñoz's investigation only because I thought it might help me defend my client. I still am, maybe even more so, even though I have effectively switched clients.

When I get to the jail, Pete Stanton is waiting for me. Dispensing with hello, he simply says, "I made the arrest."

"Why?"

"We got a request from a sister law enforcement agency. It was going to happen, so I figured it was best if I did it."

Pete's making the arrest was actually a kind gesture; he knew Sam would find it slightly less intimidating if he did so. "Has he been booked?" I ask.

"Yeah. You can see him now."

"I need to check in and go through the process."

He shakes his head. "Not today you don't; I took care of it." With that, he motions to the sergeant behind the desk, who nods his assent.

"Thanks."

I'm led into an anteroom, where Sam is waiting for me. He has a cuff on one wrist, and the other end is attached to the table. Seeing it really pisses me off.

"Andy, am I glad to see you. What the hell is going on?" His voice is surprisingly calm, without any trace of panic or anger. He just seems bewildered, which gives him something in common with his attorney.

I tell him everything Judge Hurdle told me, and I watch his confusion grow. "Why would Denise do that? Why would she lie like that? It doesn't make sense."

"Is it all a lie, Sam?" It's a question I have to ask, so I don't make a wrong move.

"What do you mean? Come on, you think I could murder someone?"

"Of course not. That's not what I was talking about. Were you and Denise Price ever intimate?"

"Absolutely not. Andy, I need you to fix this. You have to find out what the hell is happening and get me out of here as soon as possible. I've got some money; I'll pay whatever your fee is."

"This one's on the house," I tell him, though I don't mention a problem that I just recognized. The fact that I was representing Denise, who has now accused Sam and myself, creates a whole boatload of conflicts that could interfere with my ability to represent Sam. It's a problem I'm going to have to deal with, and quickly.

Then I think of still another problem, in what I'm sure will be an endless list. "Sam, where's your computer?" If the prosecutor gets his hands on it and sees Sam's efforts to delve deeply into Barry's finances, it's a disaster, legal and otherwise.

"In the bunker."

"Does anyone know about that place other than you and the team?"

"No."

"Good." I make a note to call the Holiday Inn and give them my credit card information, so the computer can stay in that room as long as we want.

"What about Crash?" Sam asks.

It takes me a moment to realize he's talking about his dog. "Where is he?"

"At my house."

"I'll check into it. Most likely they took him to the shelter."

Sam starts to literally moan, so I continue. "Don't worry. You can imagine how well Willie and I know the people down there. I'll get Crash out and he can stay at my house."

"Thanks, Andy. The thought of him in a cage drives me crazy."

It's not a good time to point out the irony that Sam himself is about to spend a lot of time in a cage. And the thought of that drives me crazy.

Security would have been heavy anyway. It's just a fact of modern life: politicians are more carefully guarded than they used to be. Special Agent Muñoz always viewed it as people being protected at a level inversely proportional to their competence.

But an event like the Northeastern Governors' Conference would have called for a very substantial law enforcement presence in any case. Twelve governors were to attend the event, which moved each year on a rotating basis. This particular year it was being held in Augusta, Maine.

There was no way the Augusta police force was prepared to handle the responsibility on its own. As was typically the case at these conferences, the state police bore the brunt of the load, with federal help if requested.

But this time it didn't have to be requested. Though there was no hard evidence of a specific threat, the pieces of the puzzle that Muñoz was dealing with worried him.

Murders linked to talk of assassinations had taken place in the state capitals of Maine and New Hampshire, and now that Ohio had been indirectly added to the group, Muñoz's concern was heightened. The chief executives of each of those states would be together at the conference, which made it something of a target-rich environment.

So Muñoz received permission to heavily inject the FBI into the security assignment, and more than thirty agents descended on Augusta. He understood that it wasn't really logical. If the governors were to be targeted in Maine, then the men chosen to be the assassins made little sense. For example, if they were going to try to kill the governor of New Hampshire while he was in Maine, why would it have been necessary to hire an assassin from that governor's hometown?

But neither Muñoz nor his bosses had any desire to wind up with a bunch of dead governors, so every precaution would be taken. A meeting was called of all the participating agencies, and a strategy was agreed upon.

Maine State Police would remain the lead agency, but they and everyone else were aware that the feds would be calling any important shots that needed to be called. The individual governors, their staffs, and their own security details were all updated and brought into the process, and all agreed to exercise more vigilance than usual.

The conference was scheduled to last just thirty-six hours, and they proved to be just about the most blissfully boring thirty-six hours that Muñoz and his colleagues had ever spent.

Absolutely nothing of consequence happened, and at least during the meetings Muñoz sat in on, that included the political discourse as well. But there was no danger — no incidents, no arrests, and not even an angry word during the entire time.

The makeshift law enforcement unit disbanded once all the politicians were out of town. To a person, they were relieved that it had proved to be a false alarm.

Muñoz had no way of knowing if the obvious internal strife among the bad guys, which had led to so many murders, had forced them to call off their plans. There was simply no evidence that he and his colleagues had dodged a bullet, or that one was ever planned to be fired.

But if those bullets were eventually going to be fired, it would be up to Muñoz to find out where and when, and to make sure they missed.

Been here, done this. I've already sat in this courtroom dealing with the legal system's efforts to convict the murderer of Barry Price, and now I'm here again. But now Sam is sitting next to me at the defense table, so as the movie tagline said, "This time it's personal."

Little else is different. Hike is also with me, and across from us Thomas Bader sits with what looks like his same team. Since the Denise Price bombshell, Bader has been decidedly more adversarial toward us. Whatever his pretense was for pretending to be Mr. Cooperative, he's dropped it.

When the same bailiff announces that Judge Calvin Hurdle is presiding, it feels like I've already seen this movie. I can't say I liked it the first time.

The very unusual situation concerning Denise Price and her allegations has taken an already high-profile case and increased it a few media notches. The gallery today is packed, and I recognize a number of television journalists. I even declined an invitation to appear on the *Today* show this morning.

"Mr. Bader, I understand you have an issue to bring before the court?" Judge Hurdle says.

Bader stands, buttoning his jacket as he does, as if speaking with an unbuttoned jacket would be a major faux pas. "Your Honor, I'm afraid there is a serious and unresolvable conflict here. Mr. Carpenter has already represented a client accused of this same crime. To take on a new client is a clear conflict. We believe that Mr. Willis must employ different counsel and should do so in a timely manner."

Sam stiffens as he hears what Bader has to say. I should have warned him that it was coming, but I didn't get to talk to him before we started.

"Your Honor, I am no longer counsel for Denise Price. She has made allegations against me, and they will be investigated and determined to be completely unfounded. That in no way should prevent Mr. Willis from representation by the lawyer of his choosing."

Judge Hurdle looks a little dubious and

asks, "What is your position regarding privileged communications between yourself and Mrs. Price?"

I nod. "It is my understanding from Your Honor that Mrs. Price has revealed what she purported to be privileged conversations that she and I had. By doing so, our position is that she waived any and all privileges. However, I have no intention of using any of those communications in this trial."

"Mr. Bader?"

"Your Honor, this is a classic conflict, and it is exacerbated by the fact that Mrs. Price at this point remains a defendant. Her rights would not be adequately protected if Mr. Carpenter were to represent Mr. Willis against the same charge."

I shake my head in disdain at Bader's comment, trying to conceal my worry. "Mrs. Price's jury will not be sitting here, and I have no doubt that Your Honor will be able to impanel a fair and unbiased jury in both cases. Mr. Willis's rights must not be sacrificed by a purely hypothetical and unfounded concern for someone else's."

Bader doesn't chime in, so I fill the silence. "The rights that we should be concerned with here belong to the person who stands accused, who sits at this table. If there was a conflict, it would be he who could be damaged by it. It is clearly a waivable situation, Your Honor."

There are two kinds of conflicts, waivable and nonwaivable. My hope is that Judge Bader will recognize that this situation is the former.

He does.

He reads a small speech explaining the situation to Sam and asks if he fully understands what he has just heard.

"Yes, Your Honor," says Sam.

"And is it your desire to fully and completely waive your claims in this matter and retain Mr. Carpenter as your counsel?"

"Yes, Your Honor," says Sam.

"Very well. Mr. Carpenter, welcome back."

I smile. "Thank you, Your Honor, always a pleasure. Now, if it please the court, I would like to make a request."

"Proceed."

"Thank you. At this point, the defense would ask that Your Honor grant us a preliminary hearing so that we can face these charges."

Out of the corner of my eye, I can see Bader react in surprise. As requests go, he would have considered it more likely that I would ask for a change of venue to Pluto.

It's accepted wisdom that the defense does not want a preliminary hearing, because it's almost always a losing effort. The prosecution wins going away, and the resulting publicity is bad for the defendant. The standard of proof for the prosecution is so low that they rarely even present their whole case.

The judge asks Bader for comment, and he's quick to do so. "Your Honor, a sitting grand jury is going to hear the evidence tomorrow." Most often preliminary hearings are not held, and a grand jury issues the charges. I'm trying to change that here.

I nod. "Then it's lucky we're talking about this today. Sam Willis is an innocent man; until now he has never been convicted of a crime or even charged with one. Then suddenly, because of a single unsubstantiated allegation by a person who last week Mr. Bader was arguing was a lying murderer beyond a reasonable doubt, he finds himself sitting in a prison cell, facing incredibly serious charges."

Bader shakes his head. "They are not unsubstantiated; there is ample evidence to hold the defendant for trial."

"I have not seen that evidence. Sam Willis has not seen that evidence. So rather than Mr. Bader present it in secret, let him do it in the light of day, where we can challenge it and demonstrate the injustice that is being done."

I'm giving speeches, playing to the media people, who must be eating it up. Bader is in a very difficult position. He has the legal right to adamantly refuse our request, but he is smart enough to know if he does so, the media reaction will be decidedly negative.

Additionally, he has little to fear. He clearly feels that his evidentiary case is strong, so what's wrong with letting the world, including future jury members, hear about it?

I continue. "Your Honor, Sam Willis's accuser sits in jail as we speak, accused of the same homicide. Is it the prosecution's intention to just keep arresting people for the murder of Barry Price until they happen to hit on the right one?"

Bader is getting angry, which happens to be the emotional state I prefer for my legal adversaries. "Your Honor, that is a gross mischaracterization of the situation."

"Maybe it is," I say. "Let's find out. Let's let everyone find out. If the prosecution has nothing to hide, let them demonstrate it by coming out in the open. What have they to lose?"

I'm not even sure Bader heard what I said; he's in rather animated consultation with two of his colleagues.

"Mr. Bader?" Judge Hurdle prompts.

Bader doesn't respond. He's still huddling, so the judge once again tries to get his attention, a little more sternly this time. "Mr. Bader?"

He finally stops talking to his staff and faces the judge. "Sorry, Your Honor. The prosecution would be willing to proceed with a preliminary hearing at the time of your choosing."

The judge accepts that and we've officially won the argument. It will be a while until we find out if that's a good thing.

As soon as the hearing is adjourned, Bader comes over to me. "They told me you were unpredictable," he says.

"Most people find it charming."

"Really? It must be an acquired taste. See you in court."

With that, he turns and walks away. It's a precision turn, like someone with a rifle on his shoulder would do during close-order drills.

I've got a feeling that Mr. Bader is no longer one of the great Andy Carpenter's legion of fans.

I request some time to meet with Sam

before he is taken back to the jail. He's a little shaken by the close call in court and bewildered by my preliminary hearing request. Add that to the fact that he is suddenly spending his time in a seven-by-ten-foot cell, and he's had a bit of upheaval in his life.

"Sam, it wasn't a spur-of-the-moment decision, but it was close."

"What was your reasoning?"

"Basically I wanted to shake things up. And I wanted to let the world know that we're here and not going to put up with months of this crap."

He smiles. "Music to my ears."

I caution him that there's little chance we will win and thereby get the charges dropped, but that I think we will benefit from the process.

"I'm in your hands," he says, which gives me an even bigger pit in my stomach than I usually get from knowing a client's life is in my hands. I'm told that some defense attorneys like that feeling of power; if they do, they should be institutionalized.

"I'll do my best."

"Andy, there's something I don't understand. How can there be evidence against me?"

"We'll find out when I go through the

discovery, but whatever it is, we'll prove that it's bullshit."

"Thanks. How's Crash doing?"

"Fine. He and Tara get along great." The truth is that Crash and a potted plant would get along great, because basically all Crash does is sleep and eat. That, and he lowers his head when Laurie or I walk by so we can pet him. He's lazy but adorable.

"He eating okay?"

"Like a small horse. But we're teaching him some discipline, store-bought biscuits only."

He smiles. "Laurie won't bake?"

"Not in this lifetime."

"Pet him for me for luck, okay?"

"I will, Sam," I say, not mentioning that since adopting lucky Crash, he's been wrongly imprisoned for murder.

"Hilda and Eli Mandlebaum visited me," Sam says. "They're really upset about what happened."

"Just tell them not to move your computer out of that room."

"I already did," he says.

We chat for a few more minutes. I can tell he doesn't want me to leave, but the guard is waiting for him. I once again give him the speech about not talking to anyone in the prison, but he knows the drill, so I'm not worried about it.

I told Denise the same thing a bunch of times; maybe I should have told her not to talk to the judge either. Then it hits me that maybe I should have worried as much about Denise listening as talking.

Sam is heading for the door and the waiting guard when I say, "Sam, wait a second." He stops, and I continue, "Those times that you visited Denise, did you tell her anything about our investigation?"

"Not really, just mentioned how we were making progress, that kind of thing. I was trying to keep her spirits up."

"When was the last time you saw her?"

"Three days ago."

"Do you remember the conversation?" I ask.

"I guess so . . . not word for word."

"Did you mention anything about Kyle Austin?"

He thinks for a moment. "I definitely didn't mention his name. I might have said something like we had a good lead, we were checking out a guy in Columbus who received money from the bad guys. That kind of thing."

"Okay," I say, my worst fears confirmed.

"Did I do something wrong?"

"No, you did fine," I tell him.

I think I'll leave out the part about his signing Kyle Austin's death warrant.

"I was giving Denise Price too much credit," I say.

Laurie and I are sitting on the couch listening to music. Tara's on the couch with us, and Crash is out cold on a recliner across the room. I'm not sure how he did it, but he actually got it to recline. I think for his birthday I'll get him a hammock.

I'm frustrated, because without the discovery material, there's nothing to do except sit and think. I don't think very well when I'm trying to think. Most of my best thoughts enter uninvited.

"How so?" Laurie asks.

"At first I thought she was lying about Sam and me as some kind of desperate move to help herself. I figured she thought the trial was going badly, which it was, and she'd somehow get off by implicating Sam."

"That's giving her too much credit?" Laurie asks.

"It is if I'm right about her being involved in Kyle Austin's death. I think she has access to a means of communication in the jail, probably a cell phone. According to Pete, there are more cell phones in the average prison than at a Best Buy."

"No question about that," Laurie says.

"So Sam mentions a lead in Columbus. He doesn't have to mention the guy's name, because she knows all about him. Austin immediately became dangerous to them; if we found him, he might talk. They've been eliminating a lot of people for just that reason."

"There're other places the leak could have come from."

"I'm sure that's true, but I don't think it did. I think it was Denise."

The phone rings, not my favorite thing to happen at eleven o'clock at night. The caller ID says US GOV, and I'm hoping that means it's Muñoz, whom I've been trying to reach.

It is. "You've had a rough couple of days," he says.

"I've had worse."

"When?"

"You should have seen me the year the Giants didn't make the playoffs, and don't get me started on when they stopped making red M&M's." Then, "It's my fault Austin got killed."

"How's that?" The tone of his voice moves from light to deadly serious in a nanosecond.

"Denise Austin found out that you were looking for him and got the word to her people on the outside."

"And exactly how did that happen?"

"One of my people," I say.

"Maybe you need new people."

"On the other hand, if not for my people, you'd be sitting around not knowing anything, with your thumb up your ass."

"So is that what you called me for? To tell me that you were responsible for getting a potentially key witness iced?"

"No, I wanted to tell you that nothing has changed in our arrangement. I've still got a client to defend, and you've still got bad guys to catch."

He pauses for a minute, then "Okay."

"So where are you?" I ask.

"Nowhere," he says, either lying or displaying more candor than most FBI agents this side of Cindy Spodek. "We're playing defense."

"Do the dead guys have anything in common?" I ask, referring to the murder victims in Augusta, Concord, and Columbus. "Other than the fact that they all happened to live in state capitals?"

He hesitates for a few moments before answering. "What do you mean?"

"Well, I'm not talking about whether they were in the same fraternity or all rooted for the Celtics. I mean, is there anything about them that made them particularly dangerous? Maybe a violent history?"

Another hesitation. "Yes. At least one guy in each city was a veteran."

"Is that unusual?"

"They were all artillery experts."

There is no doubt that Sam's arrest was warranted. The discovery documents confirm the depressing fact that the evidence against him, even in this early stage of the investigation, is substantial and incriminating.

The least of it is Sam's presence at the house, alone with Denise, the two times that the police showed up. When they informed Denise that Barry had died in the crash and when they came to arrest her after the service, Sam was there. It tends to support her claim that they were having an affair, though far from conclusively.

There are three bombshell pieces of evidence. One is a trace amount of botulinum toxin found on the backseat of Sam's car. Another is a similar find on his jacket, which he had worn to the party at the Price house the night before Barry's death. To fill out the dismal trifecta, a beer bottle with Sam's prints on it was found in the basement of the Price home, not far from the sink where the botulinum traces had been found.

I head down to the jail to see Sam, dreading the conversation. Even though I know exactly the kinds of things he is going to say, I have to give him a chance to say them, just in case I'm wrong.

I'm not wrong. Sam goes nuts when he hears about the evidence. To be innocent, and to hear this kind of stuff, must reach a level of infuriating that has to be excruciating.

When he calms down, he explains what must have happened, as best he can. "When I pulled up to her house, she came out to tell me that Barry had already left. She was at the passenger-side window, which I thought was a little strange but not a big deal. Then she looked in and said that the backseat was wet, and she opened the back door and reached in to wipe it off. I'll bet that's where they found the poison."

He's right about that, and I tell him so.

"She invited me in, and when I got inside, she hung up my jacket. She must have put it on the jacket then; it would have been a piece of cake. Damn, I walked right into this."

"There's no way you could have known,"

I say. "Was it the same jacket you wore to the party?"

"Yeah."

"What about the beer bottle?"

"I drank coffee when I was there the night Barry died. But then she brought out two bottles of beer, to toast old times."

"So she made sure she kept the bottle with your prints on it, just in case."

"Damn," he says, thinking about the implications of all this. "She set me up. And she killed him. She killed Barry."

"She was certainly involved in it," I say. "And a hell of a lot more."

"It's humiliating what she did to me," he says.

I don't mention that she had planned a worse end for him. Denise had planned to give Barry the botulinum toxin, which she assumed would never be discovered in his incinerated body. When she learned that Sam would be flying with Barry, she considered his death in the crash merely "collateral damage." When he didn't make the flight, she used him as a person to frame when things went bad for her.

"Andy, you're going to get me out of here, right?"

"Yes, as a matter of fact I am."

"When is the hearing?"

"Friday."

"Are we ready?"

"We will be."

He nods. "Good."

I head home to continue the process of getting ready, but first I'm going to take a walk with Laurie, Tara, and Crash. Most dogs, when you hold a leash up, go nuts and run to the door. Crash, on the other hand, barely looks up from his spot on the couch. His expression is saying, *What the hell are you doing with that thing?*

But dogs need exercise, so once again we manage to coax Crash outside. I doubt Tara is pleased, because Crash's presence means we'll be walking a lot slower than usual.

We don't talk about the case, other than Laurie asking me how Sam is holding up. "He's scared, but probably doing better than I would in the same situation." I point to Crash. "He's counting on his good-luck charm to save him."

She smiles. "Not his lawyer?"

"I am merely the conduit through which Crash works his magic."

We cut our walk short, both because I need to get back to prepare for the hearing, and because the full walk at Crash's pace would take until morning.

When we get home, the phone is ringing,

and Laurie rushes to get it. After saying "hello" and listening for a moment, she hands the phone to me.

I decide to mimic Laurie's conversational gambit and say, "Hello."

"Mr. Carpenter, this is Richard Glennon . . . from the bank."

It wasn't necessary for him to tell me where he works. I know that he is the officer at the Island Bank of the Caribbean in charge of the Imachu account. We were supposed to meet, but his boss, Randall Franklin, intervened.

"I know who you are, Mr. Glennon. What can I do for you?"

"We need to talk." His voice is a little shaky, maybe with nervousness, maybe fear. I can't tell which.

"Okay. What about?"

"Things that I know."

"When would you like to meet?" I ask, trying not to sound too eager.

"You can't tell anyone that I contacted you."

"I'm fine with that."

He doesn't seem to think that is reassuring enough. "My wife is scared to death. If they find out, they'll kill me."

"Who are 'they'?"

"I'll get back to you."

"When?" I ask.

Click.

If I've been more frustrated, I can't remember when. I don't think I said anything to scare him, but he definitely backed off. It certainly sounded like he had something important to say, and Sam and I can use whatever help we can get.

I look around for Crash and discover that he summoned up the energy to get back on the couch. I walk over and pet him on the head.

"Make him call back, Crash. Make him call back."

The media are really into this. The usual pattern, even in a high-profile criminal case, is that the arrest is made, and it is months, or in some cases more than a year, before the public gets to hear the evidence. Because in this case there is a preliminary hearing, at least some of the facts can be examined and weighed when the case still feels "fresh" to the media.

And the things we'll be talking about are right up the media alley: murder, money, sex, infidelity, betrayal. It's fair to say this stuff is more likely to make the front pages than tort reform and debt ceiling negotiations.

Bader has to make a strategic decision concerning how much of his case to present. Typically the prosecutor wants to show as few cards as possible, just enough to make sure the case proceeds to trial.

Complicating matters for him is the fact

that he really hasn't had time to put his case together. He must feel that once he's able to conduct a full-fledged investigation, he'll be in a much stronger position. But I've called his hand well before he's ready.

He also has to know I'm coming at him. I wouldn't have called for the hearing if I was just going to let his witnesses sail through. And I am, in fact, going to challenge them. But I'm going to do a lot more.

And that is something Bader couldn't possibly anticipate.

When Sam is brought into the courtroom, he seems more upbeat than at any time since his arrest. He thinks the world is finally going to hear his side of it, and in part he's correct. What he's not focusing on is that the same world is about to hear the State of New Jersey accuse him of murder.

The truth is that it's extremely unlikely I will convince Judge Hurdle to dismiss the charges. I hope that he will, but he is not really my audience here.

There's no jury in the room, so a lawyer in my position generally sticks closer to the book and eliminates the theatrics that juries might eat up but that judges frown on. But that's not how I'm going to play it, because I'm speaking to the media and the potential jurors that are out there.

Bader's first witness is Lieutenant Chuck Jennings of the Morristown Police, and Bader will likely use him to present his overall theory of the case.

"Lieutenant, were you at the Price residence on the night that Barry Price died?"

"Yes."

"What was your reason for being there?"

"I was breaking the news to Mrs. Price that her husband had been killed."

"Were you and she alone?"

"No. My partner was with me, and Sam Willis was with Mrs. Price."

"What time was this?"

"Just after eleven P.M."

"And how did Mrs. Price react to the news?"

"She became hysterical," Jennings says. "Some neighbors heard the commotion, and they came over to console her."

"What did Mr. Willis do?"

"He left."

"When and where did you next see Mr. Willis?"

"At the Price residence two days later."

"Why were you there?"

"To arrest Denise Price for the murder of her husband."

"Was she once again alone with Mr. Willis?"

"Yes."

Bader pauses a moment to let this sink in, recognizing that the public is watching. The idea that Sam seemed always to be alone with another man's wife, ultimately his widow, has to raise at least some suspicion.

"When did you next see Mrs. Price?"

"I met with her at the jail early last week."

"For what purpose?"

"She had spoken to Judge Hurdle and made some allegations, which I was going to hear and investigate."

It is here where the rules of this kind of hearing work against us. Denise has been correctly advised by her new attorney not to testify, but unlike in an actual trial, hearsay testimony is permitted. Therefore, Jennings is able to recount what Denise said as if she were in the court saying it.

He says that Denise told him that she had been having an affair with Sam, not for a long time, for less than a month. He quickly became far more invested in it than she was, and that fact worried her.

Denise was in an unhappy marriage, and she recognized that her affair was just a way of expressing her anger at Barry, while at the same time getting some of the love and attention she felt that she deserved. That was all the affair meant to her, and Denise had no intention of ever letting it become more than a brief fling.

Sam, however, was taking it much more seriously. He started to make suggestions that she leave Barry, and then became more insistent about it. She was considering breaking it off but was worried that Sam would overreact and might even confront Barry.

Then, in a conversation at the jail soon after Denise's arrest, Sam told her that she shouldn't worry, that Andy Carpenter would get her off, and then they could be together. "This had to end this way," is what Denise quoted Sam as saying, and she believed at that moment that he had killed Barry.

I believe that Denise said these things to Jennings, but it's still weird listening to him spout this nonsense about me and Sam. And it proceeds to get worse. According to Jennings, Denise said that she told me about Sam's comments and her suspicions of Sam. According to her concocted story, I told her not to tell anyone about it, that it would be better for everyone that way.

Bader beats this to death for a while longer but doesn't get into the other evidence that was subsequently found against Sam. He's going to bring forensics people in for that testimony, which makes sense. They're harder to challenge.

So basically the only thing for me to cross-examine Jennings on is his conversation with Denise, since that is all the direct testimony was about.

"Lieutenant Jennings, you said your conversation with Denise Price took place in the jail?"

"That's correct."

"She was incarcerated there?"

"Yes."

"Why?" I ask, as if I didn't know.

"She was on trial for the murder of Barry Price, her husband."

"The same Barry Price Sam Willis is accused of murdering?"

"Yes." Jennings is pretty much sneering his disdain at me.

"Did you put her there? Did you make that arrest as well?"

"Yes."

"When she later told you this story about Sam Willis and myself, you believed her?"

"I wasn't sure."

"But when you subsequently sought a search warrant for Mr. Willis's house, based solely on her statements, you told a judge in writing that you believed her?"

"That's not the way it was worded; I said

that it was more likely true than not."

"Sounds like you believed her, but you weren't positive. Is that a fair way to describe it?"

He's stuck. Not to agree with that is to admit to falsifying a search warrant, something judges don't exactly view with fondness.

"Yes," he admits.

"When you arrested her for the murder, did she claim to be innocent?"

"Yes."

"Did you think that was truthful?"

"No."

"So at that time you thought she was a liar, in addition to a murderer?"

"I didn't think she was being truthful at the time."

Jennings has just given me a big opening, and his wincing slightly shows me that he knows it. "So you believe her now? You now think that when she said she didn't murder her husband, she was telling the truth?"

He's in a tough spot. Denise is still in prison, charged with the murder. If the arresting officer says under oath that she was being truthful when she proclaimed her innocence, it would be devastating for that prosecution.

"I'm not sure."

"You have a reasonable doubt?" I hate helping Denise this way, but this line of questioning also helps Sam.

"I'm not sure."

I nod, as if I now understand. "I get it. So you think she might be a liar and a murderer, but you think she was telling the truth about Mr. Willis."

He doesn't want to defend himself by saying that they've uncovered other evidence, because it would then open the door for me to ask about it.

"I believe she was telling the truth about Mr. Willis" is his lame, unexplained response.

"Did you consider the possibility that she was trying to blame Mr. Willis in the hopes of saving herself from prosecution? Any chance that entered your mind?"

"I certainly considered it."

"If you think a liar and a murderer trying to talk her way to freedom is somebody worthy of being believed, is there anyone on the planet you wouldn't believe? If Charles Manson said he was surfing on the day of the Tate murders, would you have asked to borrow his surfboard? Did Lee Harvey Oswald just feel like taking in a movie?"

Bader objects, and even with the relaxed standards of this hearing, Judge Hurdle sustains and tells Jennings not to answer.

"Are you planning any other arrests for this murder?" I ask. "Because you could be heading for a record."

Bader objects again, so I just add, "Lieutenant, in this day and age, it's refreshing to find such a trusting person."

Sergeant Darren Leonard is something of a bit player in this. He merely executed the search warrants on Sam's apartment, car, and office, after Denise had implicated him. Bader is simply using him to describe the actual mechanics of the procedure.

His direct testimony takes less than twenty minutes. He entered the house with a team of forensics people, who did their work while he set about to collect any documentary evidence he could find. To that end, he found nothing whatsoever, which Bader took to be incriminating in and of itself.

"Did you impound Mr. Willis's personal computer?" he asks.

"No. We couldn't find it."

"In neither his office nor his home?"

"That's correct."

"Did you ask him where it was?"

"Yes. He told me it was none of my business."

There's little for me to do with him on cross-examination, but that doesn't mean I'm not going to try.

"Sergeant Leonard, did you take any of Mr. Willis's clothing back to the lab as a result of your search?"

"We did."

"What items did you take?"

"A winter jacket, a pair of pants, two shirts, and a pair of shoes."

"Did you just choose those items at random?"

"No, we were looking for them specifically."

"Really? Why?"

"My understanding is that Mrs. Price said that's what Mr. Willis was wearing the night of the party at their house."

"So they had upward of fifty people over to a party, and Mrs. Price remembered each item of clothing that one of those guests was wearing, many weeks later?"

"That's what she said."

"Very impressive. Do you remember what you were wearing last Monday night?"

He grins. "Can't say as I do."

"Did Denise Price tell you where in the car to search as well?"

"No, sir."

"Did you find any incriminating evidence

306

in either Mr. Willis's home or car other than what Denise Price pointed you to?"

"No, sir."

"Thank you."

None of what I've accomplished so far is going to carry the day for Sam. The media reports have me making more progress than I am, because they're paying more attention to the sport of it than the legalities.

The overwhelming advantage in this case is with the prosecution. Judges almost always allow these cases to go on to trial so that a jury can decide. For us to win, we have to score repeatedly, spike the football each time, and then hang Bader from the goalposts.

Of course, we haven't sprung our surprise yet, and its success or failure will tell the tale. What bothers me is that our chances are somewhat reliant on things out of my control.

One of the most important of those things is Richard Glennon's contacting me again and telling me the information he dangled in our last conversation. He sounded scared, so I don't want to press him yet, because there is a chance it would push him farther away.

Mr. Glennon, please pick up the phone.

The materials were ready and in storage. The assembly of the various parade floats, as well as the podiums and bleachers for the speechmaking, wouldn't begin for another week and would take three days. A similar effort was made every year, so it had become very efficient. Yet it was still a lot of work for something that would be disassembled after twenty-four hours.

The Los Angeles parade would begin in Griffith Park, where a large crowd would assemble and the speeches would be given. Every politician of consequence would be there. There was no way they would miss a chance to publicly praise the troops and honor those who had lost their lives in service.

Some of the tributes would be sincere and heartfelt, and some less so. But participating in the event, vowing undying support for the U.S. military, was an absolute must to maintain political viability. It was okay to vote to cut funds for veterans' health care, but don't dare miss a chance to jump on the Memorial Day bandwagon.

So the platforms would be built, the sound system would be installed, and the stands would be erected. There was no concern about the weather; after all, this was Los Angeles in late May.

For Carter's men, it was the perfect venue. It was out in the open and therefore not really presenting any kind of challenge. And with the easy exits from the park, getting out would be relatively simple, especially amid the chaos that was sure to ensue.

They had long ago recorded the coordinates of where the stand would be. The van would be two thousand yards away, but with the accuracy of the guidance system, it was the same as point-blank range.

The governor, the mayor, seven congressmen and -women, and fourteen elected members of city and state government had already committed to be there. As Carter read in the media about each new politician who had decided to attend, his delight increased.

This wasn't going to be just a targeted killing; it was more a targeted mass killing.

And it was only one of fifteen such mass

killings that Carter's men were planning across the country.

Janet Scarborough is the head of the Morris County crime lab. She's probably in her early sixties, plain looking but with a warm smile. Definitely the kindly grandmother type, but give her a microscope and she becomes a defense attorney assassin.

The crux of Bader's case, at least at this point, is the forensics. Motive is where he is weakest, which is the whole area of the alleged affair between Sam and Denise Price. I'm sure he thinks that by the time of trial he'll have it all nailed down, but for now he is relying on the science. It's a potent weapon.

Scarborough conducted all the tests and has the credibility to make the results stand up. Since she's been doing this for a very long time, I'm sure she has had occasion to testify in Judge Hurdle's courtroom before, and he no doubt respects her.

Bader takes her through her experience,

then the techniques she used to run the tests on the evidence in this case. All of that takes awhile, though less time than Bader would drag it out in front of a jury. There is no need to educate Judge Hurdle; he's heard this kind of stuff many times.

"And in both cases the results were positive for botulinum toxin?" he finally asks.

She nods. "They were."

"Trace amounts?"

"I would describe them as more than trace amounts. There was more on the jacket sample than the one from the car seat, but both were fairly significant positives."

Not satisfied with that, he has her demonstrate, in terms of parts of the toxin per hundred, the difference between what she would consider trace amounts and the amounts in this sample. The math, as she presents it, is very clear. This was a fairly significant amount of concentrated, deadly poison.

"Could this be considered in any way commonplace?" Bader asks. "Might these kind of toxins be found frequently in our environment, and we just don't realize it?"

She shakes her head. "No. Botulinum is a natural toxin, in that it comes from food and is found in soil. But I would venture to say that you could randomly test thousands of jackets and millions of car seats and not find this kind of concentration."

He turns her over to me for cross-examination.

"Ms. Scarborough, how would you carry botulinum toxin around?"

"I'm not sure I know what you mean," she says.

"Okay, you're invited to a party, and you don't know what to bring. But you can't stand the host, so you think to yourself, maybe I'll just bring some botulinum."

Bader objects and Hurdle admonishes. But the gallery laughs, and that's who I'm playing to.

Even Scarborough smiles. "I generally bring wine. But if I had occasion to transport botulinum toxin, it would probably be in a secure test tube, inside a sealed, airtight, waterproof carrier."

"Anything else would be unsafe, correct?"

"In my opinion, yes."

"And if you were to lay that carrier on the seat of a car or have it brush against your jacket, there would be no transference of the toxin, correct?"

"Correct."

"So someone who knew the deadly properties of that toxin, someone who possibly even acquired it and planned to kill with it, would always handle it in a safe way, as you would, correct?"

"I would hope so, but I couldn't say for sure what someone else might do."

I nod. "Fair point. So let's say, hypothetically, that someone wasn't nearly as careful as you are, and he or she carried it in a container so insecure that it leaked onto the backseat of a car and onto the person's jacket. Are you with me?"

"Yes."

"Good. Now the prosecution's theory is that person literally took the botulinum to a party, and in the process it got on the backseat of his car and his jacket. If that was true, wouldn't it also be elsewhere?"

"What do you mean?"

"Well, he wouldn't likely carry it in front of him. Wouldn't some be in his pockets or elsewhere on his clothes?"

"That's certainly possible."

"If the container was so porous that it leaked in the car, wouldn't it have had to spread elsewhere?"

"I couldn't say."

I frown, trying to show that she is avoiding the obvious truth. "But it doesn't make a lot of sense, does it?"

"No, it doesn't."

"Let me try another hypothetical, and you

tell me if this would be more likely, speaking only scientifically. Suppose someone wanted to make it appear as if the defendant used the toxin, and to do so, that person deliberately put some on his car seat and his jacket when he entered the party and took it off. Is there anything scientifically incorrect about that scenario?"

"Not scientifically, no."

"Thank you, no further questions."

The court day has gone fine; even Hike gives me the thumbs-up. But the best moment of the day comes on the way home, when my cell phone rings, and Richard Glennon is on the line.

"Mr. Carpenter," he says, "I'm ready to talk."

Denise Price was growing angrier by the minute. It had all started out so well for her. Once she had made the determination that the trial was going badly, she took the decisive action of putting Plan B into effect. She thought that it should have been the original plan, but she was not the one calling the shots.

Once she spoke to the judge and told the new story, however, things took an immediate turn for the better. A mistrial was declared, depriving the twelve cretins on that jury from deciding her fate.

She didn't have to hire another lawyer, one just showed up, courtesy of her friends. He seemed really confident and didn't keep warning her not to be too optimistic too soon, like Carpenter did.

She was proud of herself, the way she planned for all contingencies, even though in some cases she was just following directions. The biggest piece of luck was when Sam showed up late that night, having hit the dog.

She had heard only a few hours earlier that Barry had invited Sam on the flight. She had been somewhat concerned that he'd be able to take the controls when the poison hit Barry, but the dog sealed Barry's fate. It also provided a backup person to blame for the murder.

Poor, stupid Sam.

Her new lawyer told her she'd be out of jail in no time, that in return for testifying against Sam, the charges would most likely be dropped. At the very least, according to the lawyer, she'd get bail.

But it hadn't happened, at least not yet. He kept claiming it was about to be finally resolved, but there was always an excuse. And meanwhile, she was in this humiliatingly awful place, surrounded by criminals.

Except for when she had visitors, she was allowed only two hours a day out of her cell, for exercise and to spend time in the common area. She barely used that time, preferring to be in her cell. She had enough "social interaction" during mealtimes, when they served that garbage that they referred to as food.

Her lawyer was due to come in that

evening, just after six o'clock, and she was going to read him the riot act. She'd give him forty-eight hours to get her out or she was getting another lawyer, one who knew what he was doing.

Denise went to dinner at the appointed time; she was hungry and would see if there was anything worth eating. She nibbled on some tuna salad, sitting as far away from the other inmates as she could manage. She took some pleasure in noting to herself that she was probably worth more money than everyone in the crowded room put together.

On the way back to her cell, there was a commotion, with inmates milling about and angry words being yelled. She tried to avoid the crowd, but it seemed to move toward her, and she found herself in the middle of a bunch of obvious lunatics.

Even with the aid of surveillance cameras, there was no way to tell who put the ice pick through Denise's heart, but it was still there when she hit the floor, already dead.

She was going to miss the meeting with her lawyer.

I don't want to appear desperate, and I certainly don't want Glennon to hear me salivating all over my cell phone.

"I'm ready whenever you are. What are we going to talk about?"

"I know it all. Barry Price, Donald Susser, Augusta . . . I know who they are and what they're planning to do. I'm afraid I had a part in it."

"I understand," I say, though there's a good chance I don't. I assume the fact that he actually sent the wire transfers means he's afraid he's committed a crime. He may or may not be right, depending on what he knew.

"Then you need to help me. I don't want to go to jail. I'm a married man; I want to have a family." He sounds frantic.

Now it makes sense that he's calling me rather than the police; he wants to be my client. Just what I need, more clients.

"Let's talk," I say, "and I'll do everything I can. Where would you like to meet?"

"I don't know; it can't be in public. If they find out . . . you don't know what these people are like."

"Do you have a car?"

"Yes."

I tell him we can meet at the pavilion near the sports fields in Eastside Park in Paterson. It's only about a half hour from the city and easy for him to find.

The good news is that I'm obviously very familiar with it; in fact, I've arranged similar clandestine meetings there with nervous informants in the past. The bad news is that none of those meetings went particularly well.

But he seems fine with it, and we set the time at ten o'clock tomorrow night. The best part is that he doesn't insist that I come alone. I doubt there's any danger, but I've been wrong before, and I'll bring Marcus just in case.

Actually, if I were Richard Glennon, I'd probably be buying as much term life insurance as I could find. Whether it's the three guys in Augusta or Kyle Austin in Columbus, association with Andy Carpenter seems to put people down rather low on the actuarial table.

When I get home, Laurie calls Marcus and makes sure he can be there. Then she and I take Tara and the canine dynamo to that same Eastside Park for a walk. We don't go down to the lower level, where the meeting will be held, but we don't need to. I'm very familiar with it.

"He wants immunity," I tell Laurie. "I'm pretty sure of it."

"He won't get it if he has blood on his hands."

"I don't think there's any actual blood involved in wire transferring. My best guess is they compromised him and then used him. But we'll know tomorrow."

"If you represent him in any way, you'll be playing a lot of roles in this case," she says.

It's something that worries me; I'd be taking conflicts to something of an extreme. "If it comes to that, I can sever Hike from our team, and he can represent Glennon."

When we get back, Marcus is waiting for us in the living room. The house was locked, and there is no sign of a break-in, so I have no idea how Marcus got in. And I'm not about to ask.

Laurie explains the setup to him. His eyes are open, so I don't think he's asleep, but he has absolutely no reaction. Finally, at the end, she asks, "Any questions?"

"Nunh," he says, proving that he's really energized by all this after all.

I use this time to read the background information on Glennon that Sam and his team put together. It might help in my dealing with him.

The file is fairly complete, but when I'm finished I go on the computer myself, to see if I can find anything additional about him. However, the only Richard Glennons I can find are a Roman Catholic cardinal and a navy rear admiral, both of whom died in the 1940s. I don't think I'll be seeing either of them in Eastside Park tomorrow night.

I won't be seeing Marcus there either. It's his style to stay completely out of sight while simultaneously managing to have the entire place surrounded. I've learned to have total confidence in him, even in situations where I think there is substantial danger.

I don't think this will be one of those times, but there's always a chance.

Everything in this case seems to be happening twice. The bailiff comes over to talk with me as soon as I arrive in court and tells me that the judge wants to see me. The only difference is that Bader is seated at the prosecution table, and the bailiff goes over to him and gives him what must be the same message. We both get up and head for the judge's chambers.

"Mr. Bader," the judge begins, "I expect you know this already, because of your position."

Bader nods, apparently knowing exactly where the judge is going but not interrupting him on the way there.

"But I am officially telling both of you that Denise Price was murdered outside the prison dining hall yesterday. She was stabbed through the heart."

I'm certainly not happy to hear this, but I'm not going to take too long to get over my devastation. "Have they caught the person who did it?"

"Mr. Bader?" the judge asks. "Do you have updated information on that?"

"No one has been apprehended, Your Honor. My sense is that no one should anticipate an arrest any time soon, if ever. It would require someone coming forward and informing."

"I don't see this as having any effect on this hearing," I say, and both of them agree. The truth is that it might have a significantly positive effect for us if it goes to trial. Denise will obviously not be there to testify, and Lieutenant Jennings likely won't be able to provide her hearsay testimony, as he did under the less strict rules of a preliminary hearing.

We head back out into the hearing room, and I tell Sam what has transpired. He seems really upset by the news, which is pretty amazing. Denise is one hundred percent responsible for the horrible situation in which he finds himself, and he's reacting like they were just days away from going to the fraternity formal.

Today is pretty much wrap-up day for Bader. He brings in three friends of Denise, all of whom say that she was having an affair, though none are aware of who it was.

It's circumstantial evidence against Sam at this point, and barely that. Bader had better have something a lot more specific than this if we wind up going to trial.

I take it easy on these witnesses, merely asking enough questions to reemphasize the fact that they have absolutely no information tying Denise's alleged affair to Sam. I also point out that they believe Denise's affair had lasted for a number of months, whereas she told Jennings that she was seeing Sam for only one month.

The only way to resolve this discrepancy is either that she was lying about Sam or she also had other affairs. They both play well for us, especially the former.

Bader's last witness is Sergeant Ben Thompson, a prison guard for twenty-two years. He is responsible for the visitors' room at the prison, and he testifies that Sam visited her on six different occasions.

"Was he her most frequent visitor?" Bader asks.

"Yes, by far. Even more than her lawyer."

"Did you notice anything unusual between them?"

"I'm not sure what you mean by unusual," he says. "She would occasionally put her hand on his or touch his arm. That kind of thing."

When it's my turn, I start with, "Sergeant Thompson, when you saw this physical contact that you describe between Mr. Willis and Mrs. Price, did you put a stop to it?"

"No."

"So you didn't consider it improper?"

"No. Not really."

"You've seen that kind of thing before?"

"Sure."

"Sergeant, where did you go to high school?"

"Montclair High."

"Are you still friendly with any of your classmates from back then?"

"Yes. We get together all the time."

"If one of them was charged with a crime, and you were sure he was innocent, might you visit him in jail while he was on trial? Would you consider supporting him in that way?"

Thompson doesn't hesitate. "I sure would."

"Thank you," I say.

Bader rests his case, and Judge Hurdle asks me if I will be presenting witnesses. "Yes, Your Honor."

"Can you provide their names to the court?"

"Not at this point, Your Honor, I'm sorry. We're working as fast as we can to put it

326

together."

Bader objects, but the defense gets a lot of leeway in preliminary hearings, partially because of the very limited time we have to prepare.

I promise the judge I will have a list on Monday morning when we resume, and say that if Bader then needs some time to prepare, the judge can issue a continuance. There is as much chance of that happening as the judge handing out tickets to the lawyers for a Justin Bieber concert. Judges have an inbred hatred for delays of any kind.

I'm once again reasonably pleased with how the day went, though my meeting tonight with Glennon in Eastside Park will determine just how good the day really is.

At first Carter was annoyed. Since the situation with the locals in New Hampshire, Maine, and Ohio had been cleaned up rather violently, the operation had proceeded with remarkable precision. Yet now, when it was so close to bearing fruit, his superior officer was suddenly asking for all the details.

It was ridiculous. If he was going to be seriously questioned, it should have been during the strategic preparation, when substantive changes could have been made. At this late date, other than slight revisions, it was either proceed or abort, and no one was prepared to abort.

But along with the annoyance, Carter felt more than a little pride. It was a masterful plan, followed by what to this point was a masterful execution. They were making history, and no one had any right to be one-tenth as proud as Carter.

But the money people had to be given their due. For all of Carter's brilliance, he could not have come close to pulling this off without the unlimited funding he had been provided. And the truth is that they were also making him rich beyond his wildest dreams.

So he put all the relevant information on computer disks and prepared a PowerPoint presentation to show his superior when he arrived. Such was the detail that the presentation could continue for many, many hours, but Carter doubted that would be necessary.

His assumption was that his audience would quickly understand that Carter had done everything there was to do, prepared everything there was to prepare, and left nothing to chance. He figured that within an hour his superior would smile and tell him to continue on exactly as he had been doing.

The knock on the door came at eight o'clock. Carter let him in, and other than a brief acknowledgment, no other words were spoken. Neither of them was prone to chit-chat.

Carter's guest requested a beer before they begin, and it was while Carter was getting one from the refrigerator that he felt the gun against the back of his skull.

"What the hell is going on?" Carter asked as his mind raced for a way out of his predicament.

The superior laughed. "You're familiar with targeted killings, aren't you?"

"I've been loyal," Carter said. "I've given you what you wanted."

"I'm sure you have. Now I'll take it from here."

"We're on the same side; let's talk about this."

But the man holding the gun had little time to talk and none to waste. Yesterday Denise Price was eliminated, and now Carter. But his work tonight was not finished.

Richard Glennon was next.

When I was fourteen, I kissed Tina Stahlman in Eastside Park. It was easily the high point of my early formative days in the park, and my recollection is that Tina was formed pretty well by then too. Even though she subsequently and repeatedly denied the event to friends, it has remained in my mind a rare but major triumph.

My other early park days were marked by fairly consistent failures on the baseball diamonds; I was a pitcher and shortstop, but I could neither hit nor throw a curveball. I also played cornerback here on our fraternity football team, where I earned the nickname "Toast," because I was so frequently burned by opposing wide receivers.

My adult years here have been a mixed bag. There have been the always pleasant walks with Tara and Laurie, mostly during daylight hours.

I've had a few clandestine nighttime meetings with people relating to cases I've been working on. They haven't gone so well: a car blew up, a guy got splattered on my windshield, a couple of violent deaths. Businesswise it's fair to say that Eastside Park hasn't been my good-luck conference room.

Of course, the mere prevention of death, mine or anyone else's, is not going to be good enough tonight. If Glennon can give me a road map to what the hell is going on, it will be perfectly timed to fit in my strategy on how to get Sam off.

I arrive at the designated meeting place at nine forty-five. I prefer being the first to arrive, though I'm not sure why. It might be because it gives me the chance to get used to the darkness and the silence, which are not two of my favorite things. I also like to see the other person arriving, and better yet, I want Marcus to see the other person arriving.

Of course I haven't seen Marcus since last night, when he was emptying our refrigerator. I know he's here, and even though I don't think Glennon presents any danger, I'm glad that he is.

There is a winding road that leads down from the upper part of the park to the lower part, where I'm waiting. As kids we called it Dead Man's Curve, though to adult eyes it looks somewhat less fearsome.

The directions I gave Glennon included coming down that way, even though there is another entrance into the lower level of the park. So it is that road that I keep my eyes on, watching for car lights coming around the bend.

By ten fifteen I'm getting concerned that those lights are not going to appear, and by ten thirty I'm pretty sure of it. I guess I shouldn't be surprised; Glennon seemed scared to the point of being unstable.

I take out my cell phone to see if perhaps he had called and the phone didn't ring due to weak service in the park. But there are three bars and no message on the phone.

I stick it out until ten fifty and decide to leave. Glennon has my number and can certainly call if he's running late and still wants to meet. I'm not holding my breath.

I yell out, "Marcus, we're outta here!" but he doesn't answer. Marcus sticks to the script; he maintains radio silence even without radios.

I start walking toward my car, once again checking my cell phone for messages. As I do so, it rings, and in the quiet night it sounds like about a thousand decibels. It scares me so much that I drop the phone. Fortunately, it lights up when it rings, so

I'm able to see it on the ground without much difficulty.

"Please be Glennon," I actually say out loud, but the caller ID removes any suspense in that regard. It isn't Glennon calling; it's Laurie.

"Andy, where are you?"

"At the park. I was waiting for Glennon, but —"

She interrupts. "He's not going to show up."

"How do you know?"

"Because he's dead."

Eastside Park strikes again.

"Marcus, now we're really outta here!"

I make the five-minute drive home, and Laurie tells me she had been watching the local news. She was probably afraid she was going to see a story about a prominent defense attorney murdered in Eastside Park, but instead the breaking news was of something that happened on Route 80.

According to police, a car containing the body of Richard Glennon was found in a ditch off the side of the highway, in Paterson. He had been shot once in the back of the head and would have certainly died instantly.

I call Pete Stanton on his cell phone to see if he can get me any more information.

When he answers, I ask if he has heard about Glennon's murder.

"I'm watching his body being loaded into a van. Why?"

"He was on his way to meet me tonight," I say.

"You remain a regular good-luck charm. Come on in and talk to me about it."

"Where are you?"

"Headed to the morgue. Glennon's wife is on the way to ID the body."

I agree to come down and talk to him, even though it will probably be a waste of time. I won't reveal much about my case, and he won't reveal much about his. But it's worth a try.

I arrive at the morgue just in time to see a uniformed officer escort a sobbing woman into the building. I wait in the reception area, and ten minutes later the same officer brings out the same woman, sobbing even harder now. My keen investigative mind tells me that she is Mrs. Richard Glennon.

Pete finally comes out, and we go outside to talk. "Any chance you caught the killer?" I ask.

"Why? You want another client? You moved up from amateur killers to professional?"

"This was a professional hit?"

"No doubt. Now suppose you tell me why you were meeting Glennon?"

There's not really much reason for me to hold much back. The more people who are investigating all of this, the more chance there is that we'll collectively learn something.

So I tell him what I know and suggest that he call Agent Muñoz to learn more.

"You'd better hurry up and solve this," I say. "I've got a feeling something bad is about to happen."

He points back toward the morgue. "Worse than this?"

I nod. "Much worse than this."

"Your Honor, we do not have a full witness list at this time."

Bader and I are in Judge Hurdle's chambers before the start of court this morning, and Bader's reaction to my statement is predictable.

"Your Honor, this is ridiculous, and we strongly request that you put a stop to it. The defense wants to present a case, then let them present their case. But we are entitled to prepare for their witnesses."

"In the course of presenting our case, we will be demonstrating why our witness list is unavoidably not complete," I say.

Judge Hurdle frowns. "That's a little cryptic for me."

"I'm sorry, Your Honor, but my witnesses keep getting murdered."

"You mean Denise Price?" Bader asks.

"No. I would have called her, but I'm sure she would have refused to testify. I'm talking about other potential witnesses who have met the same fate."

Bader turns to Judge Hurdle in frustration. "Your Honor, he's attempting to get in witness testimony that would never have a chance of seeing the light of day in an actual trial. This is why he asked for a preliminary hearing."

I snap my fingers in mock dismay. "I'm sorry, I must have cut class the day they taught that I was required to reveal my motive for wanting a preliminary hearing. I was probably out late the night before . . . you know how that is —"

Hurdle cuts me off, which was fine, because I was pretty much finished with that speech. "Mr. Carpenter, who are your first two witnesses going to be?"

Bader's level of frustration is about to be multiplied by ten. "First, we'll be calling Lieutenant Jennings back to the stand."

"For what purpose?"

"To question him about matters that weren't brought up on direct and that I therefore couldn't cross-examine him on."

Hurdle nods; that seems reasonable. "And your second witness?"

"That will be me, Your Honor."

"Excuse me?"

"I will be testifying myself, with Your

Honor's permission."

Bader practically launches himself from his seat. "Your Honor, that is completely improper."

I shake my head. "It is not. As an officer of the court, I submit that I am the only person with knowledge of the events and substance that I will testify to. To prevent me from doing so would inhibit the search for the truth while accomplishing nothing."

"Mr. Carpenter obviously considers proper procedure and the dignity of this court to be 'nothing,' " says Bader.

I've been looking at and talking to Judge Hurdle the entire time, as if Bader is not there, and it's driving him nuts. So nuts that he just gave me an opening.

"Judge, you and I know that you are quite capable of maintaining proper procedure and the dignity of your courtroom. That isn't the issue here. The issue is whether or not Sam Willis should be deprived of his liberty and held over for trial. To do that you need all relevant information, and I am telling you, and I will demonstrate, that my testifying is the only way to get that information out there for you to consider."

Hurdle does not look convinced. "Mr. Bader?"

Bader makes an obvious effort to appear

calm and reasonable. "I would submit that Mr. Carpenter's motive here is not to ensure that the court has sufficient information. He is playing to the media and the potential jurors who are following this hearing."

I smile, as if amused by Bader's tactic. "For days now the prosecution has been presenting their own witnesses, yet I heard no concern that the jury pool out there might hear their point of view."

"That is information that they will hear at trial," Bader says. "Your fishing expedition witnesses will never get near the trial."

"I hadn't realized you had decided yet that there would even be a trial, Judge. I thought that's what this hearing was all about."

"Don't play me, Mr. Carpenter."

I nod. "Here's the reality of the situation, Your Honor. It's a preliminary hearing, so you have complete discretion as to what you will allow and what you won't allow. More important, since you will be making the final decision as to whether there is probable cause, you can listen to our case, to my testimony, and assign whatever weight to it you wish. Or give it no weight at all. It's all up to you; there is no jury here for me to unduly influence."

I continue before Bader can jump in.

"And if Mr. Bader is right, that I'm some-how playing games and interfering with the dignity of the court, then you can cut me off at any time and admonish me in front of the media that Mr. Bader suddenly seems so concerned about."

"And I will do exactly that if I deem it necessary," Hurdle says, to Bader's obvious distress. "I will also direct you to move quickly. We must adjourn early today, because the court has housekeeping issues to deal with. And as you know, we are five days from Memorial Day weekend. When we get there, this hearing had better be in my rearview mirror."

"Lieutenant Jennings, welcome back."

"Thank you," he says, but he's looking at me as if my welcome was insincere. Why must these people judge me so harshly?

"Sorry to again take you away from your important work," I say. "I'll try not to keep you long. By the way, what important work have you been doing?"

"Police work."

I give an exaggerated nod and snap of the fingers, as if I should have known better than to ask such a silly question. "Of course, police work. Because you're a policeman. What kind of police work?"

"What do you mean?"

"Well, I assume you haven't been working traffic crossings or giving out parking tickets. What have you been doing?"

"Investigative work."

"Of course," I say. "Because you're an investigator."

"Yes."

"Have you been investigating things related to this case?"

"Among others," he says.

"If we looked at the murder book and your time sheets, would we see that a good portion of that time has been on this case?"

"A good amount, not all of it."

"As I recall, Denise Price told you that she and Sam Willis had been having an affair," I say. "Do you remember that?"

"Of course."

"Have you been investigating that claim?"

He nods. "I have."

"We didn't hear anything about that in the prosecution's case, so this is your chance to add it to the record."

"What are you asking me?"

"Well, since Denise Price told you this weeks ago, what have you learned since then to support her claim that she and Sam Willis were having an affair?"

"A number of her friends have confirmed that she was having an affair."

"With Sam Willis?"

"They did not know the identity of the man. They couldn't rule him out."

"Let's start over on this one, okay? What have you learned since you spoke to Denise Price to support her claim that she and Sam

Willis were having an affair?"

"I haven't confirmed it yet. It is still a very active investigation."

"So in your very active investigation, you've come up with nothing?"

Jennings looks as if he'd like to kill me; I had better never get arrested in Morris County. "It's a process," he says.

"Thank you; I hadn't realized that. During this process, you say you've spoken to Denise Price's friends. Have you spoken to Sam Willis's friends?"

"Some of them."

"I'm going to take a wild guess that none of them told you what you were looking for. Did you search his apartment? His office?"

"Yes."

"Nothing that would confirm the affair, huh? That must be frustrating for you."

"His computer is missing."

"Aha!" I say, as if that must be the answer. "So if he sent her love letter e-mails, you wouldn't have them."

"Correct," he says, giving me an opening.

"On the other hand, you have Denise Price's computer, so you'd know if she received any. Right?"

"We have her computer."

"And you have his cell phone, on which

his e-mails are synced to his computer, right?"

"We have that, yes."

"So when you said a moment ago that you didn't have his e-mails, you were not accurately describing the situation?"

"The computer could have more on it."

"So let's recap, if we can. With all the investigative effort you have put into it, at this point Denise Price's claims of an affair with Sam Willis are completely unsubstantiated?"

"I do not yet have any direct evidence of the affair."

"What about indirect evidence? What about any kind of evidence?"

Bader finally objects, saying that I'm badgering the witness. He should have made the objection five minutes ago, but once he does, Judge Hurdle sustains it.

"So a person is in jail, facing a charge that could send her to prison for the rest of her life. She suddenly decides to tell you something that she claims she's known for months and that possibly could free her if you believe it."

Bader stands up. "Is there a question in there anywhere?"

"I'm getting there," I say, and I turn back to Jennings. "You then investigate it and turn up absolutely nothing to corroborate her claim. Yet you still refuse to believe she could have lied about it."

"The question?" Bader demands.

"Here's the question," I say. "Lieutenant Jennings, don't you think you owe Sam Willis an apology?"

"Hello, Andy. Can we come in?" Hilda asks when I answer the door.

Most evenings it might be nice to get a visit from the Mandlebaums, but this isn't one of them. Hike is over, and we're preparing for my testimony tomorrow. It's a weird sensation. In all the time I've spent in courtrooms, I have never before been on the witness stand.

"Sure, Hilda. Nice to see you. Hello, Eli."

Eli Mandlebaum is a man of few words, and he doesn't use any now, he just smiles and nods. He's holding a paper bag in front of him.

They've met Hike before, so I don't have to worry about introductions.

"We wanted to talk to you about something," Hilda says. "But first . . ." She reaches out for the paper bag, which Eli dutifully hands to her. "Can you give these to Sam?"

347

"What is it?" For all I know it could be a handgun and a bag of bullets, to help Sam escape.

"Rugelach. It's a Jewish pastry. I'm sure he's hasn't been having any."

I think it's a safe bet that Sam hasn't been sucking down rugelach in his cell. "I'll make sure he gets it," I say.

"Try one," Hilda commands, and I do. They're fantastic. They're so good that it's highly doubtful they will survive until tomorrow. Sam is going to be out of luck, since I'm pretty sure Hike and I are going to devour them when Hilda and Eli leave.

"Oh, I almost forgot," Hilda says, and she opens her pocketbook and takes out two biscuits, which she gives to Tara and Crash. "Sam gave me his recipe."

I've got to move this along. Laurie's out, so I can't dump Hilda and Eli on her. "Is this what you wanted to talk to me about?"

"Oh, no," Hilda says. "We want to tell you something about the case."

"What about it?"

"Well, before Sam . . . left, he had found another name of someone who had received wired money from that company, Imachu."

I am immediately more interested in this than in the rugelach, which is really saying something. "He never mentioned that."

She nods. "Well, maybe he forgot, because . . . he . . . he left." She seems unable to say he was arrested. "Also, we had the name, but we couldn't attach it to anything."

"What do you mean?"

"We couldn't find any information on the person other than his bank account. But Sam told us to keep working, so we have."

"And you found him?"

She nods. "Eli did."

Eli just smiles silently, as always content with life. It's Eli Mandlebaum's world; we just live in it.

"Who is he?"

"Well, the bank account was for a Mr. Miguel Cardenas, but none of the people with that name matched up. And then Eli decided to check Mike Cardenas, and bingo. Mike is English for Miguel."

It's frustrating, but Hilda tells a story at Hilda's pace.

"So we have a lot of information on him, but I thought you'd like to know where he works."

"Where?"

"At Port Newark. He's a U.S. customs manager."

"Hilda, I don't say this lightly, but the best thing about you is not your rugelach."

I get the rest of the information that Hilda

and Eli have, and then leave them with Hike. It's not a fair thing to do to them, considering what they've come up with. But I go into the other room to call Agent Muñoz. He's not available, so I leave word that I need to speak with him urgently.

He calls back within three minutes; when Andy Carpenter speaks, agents listen.

"This better be good," Muñoz says. "I'm at my daughter's dance recital."

"It's good, but first we deal."

"Don't be a pain in the ass, Carpenter."

"In my life, I think that's the sentence I've heard more often than any other. In second place is 'Kiss my ass, Carpenter.' The two are neck and neck."

"What have you got?"

"I'll tell you on two conditions. One, when you investigate it you tell me what you come up with."

"Deal, within reason," he says.

That was the easy one. "Two, you testify at the hearing on Friday."

"Kiss my ass, Carpenter."

"The gap is being narrowed," I say. "But those are my terms."

A pause, and then, "Okay, but it has to be real good."

"There's a man named Cardenas. He lives in Elizabeth, but he works in Newark. He also received wired money from the Imachu account."

"That's it?" Muñoz asks, not yet impressed and not knowing that I have a flair for the dramatic.

"Except for one thing," I say. "That job he has in Newark? It's at the port. He's a customs manager."

He doesn't say anything for a few moments, and then finally, "I've gotta go. My daughter can't dance for shit anyway."

"Are you going to testify?"

Another pause. "I'll be there Friday."

It's probably the only conversation with Hike that I've ever looked forward to. I'm sitting in the witness box, having just sworn to tell the whole truth and nothing but the truth. And Hike is preparing to take me through direct testimony.

It's amazing how different the room looks from here. I've approached witnesses hundreds of times, so I've certainly been standing near here. But somehow it's a very different perspective. It's like sitting in the first row of a theater versus sitting on the stage.

"Good morning, Mr. Carpenter."

"Good morning, Mr. Lynch."

Hike briefly takes me through my past involvement in the case, especially my representation of Denise Price. He does this for two reasons. One is to get it all in the record, even though Judge Hurdle is quite familiar with all of it. The other reason is to establish why I was involved with the situations and events I am about to testify to.

Hike asks me why I took the trip to Augusta, and I say that it was to see Donald Susser, who had contacted me and requested the meeting. "I was investigating Barry Price's murder, and I had learned that he was flying to Augusta when his plane crashed. Additionally, I was aware that Mr. Price called Mr. Susser three times in the day before he died."

"And you met with him?"

"I did, and with two of his friends. They said that they had been paid money to commit a murder, though they were not yet aware who the target was. They called it an assassination."

"Where are those men today?"

"In a cemetery. They were murdered later that night."

"To your knowledge, have the police made arrests in connection with those murders?"

"They have not. I confirmed that this morning."

Hike, as per our plan, takes me through the events in Concord and Columbus, and the details about Imachu and its bank accounts. It feels endless to me, but in fact we do it much more quickly than originally planned.

Muñoz is going to testify to basically the

same information, and it will have much more credibility and impact coming from an FBI agent. Therefore, Hike and I agreed before court began to cut our version short.

It's a calculated gamble; we're counting on Muñoz to be an effective witness. If he starts taking refuge in things being classified, or if he says that he can comment only in a very limited way on an ongoing investigation, we will be in big trouble.

More accurately put, Sam will be in big trouble.

Bader hasn't objected at all during my testimony. He seems to be trying to indicate by his posture and attitude that this is all silly and really not worthy of time and effort. But he's not about to give up the chance to cross-examine me.

"Mr. Carpenter, that's quite a story."

I smile. "Thank you. I thought I told it well."

"I'd have to go through the transcript to be sure, but in all your testimony, did you mention the murder weapon, botulinum poisoning?"

"I don't believe I did."

"With all those people you mentioned, in Augusta and Concord and Columbus and wherever, did you present any evidence that any of them killed Barry Price?"

"No. But I did point out that Barry Price's murder was just one of many."

Bader turns to Judge Hurdle. "Your Honor, please instruct the witness to only answer the questions he's asked."

"Mr. Carpenter, consider yourself so instructed."

"Yes, Your Honor."

Bader continues. "Did you place any of the people you mentioned in the house where the poison was prepared?"

"No."

"Did you present any evidence that any of those people had ever even met Barry Price?"

"No."

He smiles. "But you have my compliments. It was a really good story. No further questions."

Bader's cross-examination was very effective, and at this point in the hearing I would say that we have very little chance to prevail. I would say it, that is, if I didn't have Special Agent Muñoz coming in to testify on our behalf.

Once I'm off the stand and back at the defense table, I ask Judge Hurdle for a continuance. My request is that court not be in session tomorrow, Thursday, and resume on Friday.

"Mr. Carpenter, do you recall my mentioning that this hearing will be concluded before the holiday weekend?"

"I've committed it to memory, Your Honor, and I would not dream of doing anything to violate your wishes."

"Then why the continuance request?"

"I have only one witness remaining, and he cannot be here until Friday."

"And who might that be?"

"FBI Special Agent Ricardo Muñoz."

It's going to be a long day. I basically have nothing to do, at least as far as the preliminary hearing goes. Muñoz is my last witness, and he's not here for me to prep him on his testimony. I know what my line of questioning will be, so no further study today is necessary.

The more I think about it, even with Muñoz's testimony I'm pessimistic about our ability to prevail. I've started the process of beating myself up over my decision to ask for the prelim. I created media expectations that I don't feel I've delivered on, and that's not a good thing at all.

Muñoz is going to say the same things that I said when I testified. Even though he'll have more credibility as an FBI agent than I do as Sam's lawyer, the thrust of Bader's cross of me will hold for Muñoz as well.

We're telling a great story, but what the hell does it have to do with Barry Price?

It will drive me crazy that Sam is likely going to sit in jail, for at least a couple of months, awaiting trial. Even worse, there is no reason, at least right now, to think that we will prevail in that trial.

So I have got to dig deeper into the conspiracy that resulted in Barry Price dying on that airplane. I just wish I knew where to put my shovel. Each time that I thought I was getting close, whether with Donald Susser or Richard Glennon, they met a violent end. And they left no one behind to tell their story.

And then I realize that maybe they did. There was the woman who answered the phone when I called Donald Susser, who sounded scared and told me she probably couldn't reach him. Maybe she knows something.

Closer to home, there's Richard Glennon's wife, whom I saw at the morgue when she was identifying his body. He said she was scared, so she must have known what was going on. Maybe she knows a great deal, and maybe she has a desire to get back at her husband's killer.

I decide to start with Glennon's wife for two reasons. First of all, she's geographically closer, and I have to be here early tomorrow for the resumption of the hearing. Second, and more important, my feeling is that Susser was out on the periphery, that he was not central to whatever Barry Price was involved with.

Glennon, on the other hand, was where the money is, and I feel like this has been about the money all along. Whatever is going on, money is making it possible.

I'm not sure how to approach Mrs. Glennon. She's just lost her husband, never the best time to talk to a lawyer involved in his death. Obviously I have no standing to make her talk to me if she doesn't want to, and it seems rather unlikely that she'll want to.

I could call Pete Stanton and ask him to come along, using his position as a detective investigating Glennon's death. It wouldn't be proper, and he'd torture me in the process, but he'd probably go along with it. Pete knows and likes Sam, and certainly doesn't consider him a murderer.

I decide not to ask him to come with me. There's a chance that his presence might inhibit Mrs. Glennon from telling me what I need to know, and if I don't get anywhere with her, I can always try it again with Pete.

"I think I should go with you," Laurie says.

"Why?"

"A female presence might make her more comfortable."

"I don't make women comfortable?" I ask. "Who makes women more comfortable than me?"

"With the notable and unfathomable exception of me," she says, "have you had much luck with women in your life?"

"On second thought, maybe your coming is a good idea. My incredible manliness can be intimidating."

I once again go through the file on Glennon; included in it was an address of a home in Englewood Cliffs, New Jersey, and an apartment on Eighty-seventh Street in Manhattan.

I call Pete Stanton, who I'm sure has been dealing with Mrs. Glennon in connection with his investigation, to ask if he knows where she is.

"Why?" is his response.

"I need to talk to her."

"She hasn't suffered enough?"

"I'll be charming, and I'm bringing Laurie. But she might have information that can help Sam, so my usual waiting period to talk to grieving widows is going to have to be shortened this time."

"She's at the house in Jersey," Pete says. "I told her that would be a good idea in case we needed her to come in. I have a phone call scheduled with her in five minutes."

"It would be helpful if you could suggest she talk to me."

"Helpful to who?"

"Sam." I'm trying to take further advantage of Pete's positive feelings toward him.

Pete thinks about this for a moment. "I'll tell her that your interest is in finding her husband's killer and that talking to you might help her avoid testifying in court."

"Perfect," I say.

"I can't tell you how delighted I am to have your approval."

Click.

I wait twenty minutes and then call Mrs. Glennon. Pete has obviously spoken to her, because she says that I can come over right away, though she makes it clear she doesn't have much time to give me.

I'll take whatever I can get.

The visit by Mark Clemens was totally unexpected. Special Agent Muñoz had interviewed him twice in regard to the Price murder and its connections to the threatened assassinations, but little information had come out of those sessions.

Clemens had been calm and in command in those interviews, professing a desire to help and regretting that he was unable to really do so. But his demeanor now was different.

He was scared.

He was also, as they say, lawyered up. With him was Douglas Wagner, a prominent defense attorney in Manhattan, which showed that while Clemens might be scared, he wasn't stupid.

"My client is in possession of some information that I believe you will find valuable, and he is prepared to submit a formal proffer of that information," Wagner says.

"And in return?" Muñoz asks.

"In return he would receive immunity from prosecution."

Clemens adds, "And protection."

"Protection from what?"

"They're going to try to kill me," he says. "They're killing everyone."

According to the long-established plan, communications had already ended. Exceptions were permitted for unexpected emergencies, but the standard was that they must be mission threatening.

The men in the field had long been in place and had ample time to prepare and scout out their local field of fire. The media had unknowingly provided considerable help, broadcasting the time and route the parades would take, and more important, the specifics as to the political speeches that would be made at the conclusion.

Of course, not all the attacks would come at the respective parades' conclusions. For example, once the ones on the East Coast had been executed, and the magnitude of the disaster hit, cities in earlier time zones would immediately go into full alert, and plans would be changed.

In those cities, other plans had already

been made. In some cases the attacks would take place at the beginning of the festivities, and in others it would happen midroute. It was crucial that all attacks happen as close together as possible, to cut down on the ability of local law enforcement to anticipate and react.

But there was no scenario under which the overall impact of the day would not be devastating. The result would be that the entire power of the United States, military and civilian, would do whatever was necessary to track down the perpetrators.

Without question, some of the men in the field would be identified and arrested. That was understood by all and went with the territory.

But for those who had sent them there, those who directed the operation so brilliantly and effectively, it was a different situation entirely.

They would never be found.

Pete had successfully cleared the way. Diane Glennon is waiting for us. She is probably in her early thirties. I had never actually met her husband, only seen pictures of him, but the information I had said that he was forty-three.

She seems shaken, as certainly is to be expected. She offers us coffee, but even though I accept, she never brings it to me.

"We were very sorry to hear about your loss," Laurie says.

She nodded. "Thank you. It's still hard to process."

"Are you going to stay here?" I ask.

"Yes, I believe so. We've made so many friends."

"Mrs. Glennon, your husband was on his way to meet with me when he died. He said that he needed to tell me something, and he knew that he was in danger."

"I don't understand that," she says. "Richard was very happy. I would know if something like that was bothering him."

"So he never talked to you about something being wrong? About being worried?" In his first call to me, Glennon had said that his wife was "scared to death." Now she's claiming she had no idea about any problems.

"No, and I certainly would have known if that was the case. Richard shared everything with me."

This has thrown me off stride. I expected her to be frightened, and my goal was to pry information out of her. She is saying that there's no information to pry.

My assumption is that she's scared, and therefore lying, but I think that if I confront her directly, she'll just end the conversation. So I have to skirt around the edges.

"Was Richard happy at work? Any recent problems?"

"He was very happy there, things were wonderful. They were a very close team, always had been."

I nod, though I'm not quite buying all the wonderfulness. "I met with his boss, Mr. Sullivan, but I didn't get to meet Richard. They got along well?"

She nods. "Oh, yes. Mr. Sullivan . . . all of them."

Laurie flashes me a look like this is a complete waste of time, but I press on.

"Do you have help in making all the arrangements?"

"I'm fine, thank you," she says.

"I know Richard has two children from his previous marriage. Are they holding up well?"

She nods sadly. "Yes, but losing a parent so suddenly, it's never easy."

Laurie gives me another look, and I nod slightly. Our work here is done. We both thank her for her time and say that if there is anything we can do, or anything she remembers and wants to talk to us about Richard's last days, she should call me.

"Thank you. I'm just trying to get through this one day at a time."

When we get in the car, Laurie says, "Do you think she was lying, or scared? Or do you think her husband kept everything from her?"

I take out my cell phone. "I think this is a job for Hilda Mandlebaum."

I use the ride home to tell Laurie my developing theory, and I'm happy that she doesn't think I'm nuts. When we get home, we decide to take Tara and Crash for a walk. It takes a few minutes to get ready, because first Crash has to wake up and then stretch.

Once that is accomplished, but before we get out the door, the phone rings. It's Agent Muñoz, calling, I hope, to discuss his testimony tomorrow.

That turns out not to be it. "Can you come down to my office? We need to talk."

"Am I going to like this?"

"Let's say it will be a mixed blessing."

"According to Clemens, everybody is guilty except him," Muñoz says.

Muñoz has just told me that Clemens had been in to see him, with his lawyer. "So why did he come in?" I ask.

"To make sure he doesn't get prosecuted for the stuff he didn't do anyway and is completely and totally innocent of," Muñoz says, his sarcasm obvious. "And because he is scared shitless."

"Of being charged?"

"Yes, but that fear is currently taking a backseat to the fear that he's going to get his ass shot up."

"Why is he afraid of that?"

"Let me start from the beginning," he says. "In the world according to Mark Clemens, Barry Price was conspiring with Richard Glennon to launder money for an outside foreign entity. They didn't know what it was for or even who it was really for, but they made a lot of money doing it. Denise Price, who had an unnatural craving for money, knew about it and supported it."

"But Clemens says he had no role?"

"He knew about it but didn't stop it. Regrets that now a whole lot."

"I'm sure he does."

"It gets better. Clemens admits that he and Denise were having an affair, on and off for two years."

That's interesting information for Sam's case, since she had claimed the affair was with Sam. Of course she was apparently quite capable of carrying on with more than one guy, so the value is limited.

Muñoz continues, "According to Clemens, Barry was getting worried. Too much money was flowing through, and he was afraid he was going to get found out and arrested. So he decided to stop the money laundering."

"Which upset Denise?" I ask.

"Freaked her out."

"Enough for her to kill him?"

"Clemens says he doesn't know but that it's possible. Not only would it have cut off that particular flow of money, but she was afraid Barry was unstable and might tell what he knew in return for immunity."

"Which is why he might have been looking for a criminal attorney."

Muñoz nods. "That could have pushed her over the edge; it would have destroyed the firm and really impacted her lifestyle. But Clemens doesn't know who killed Barry. It could have been Denise, could have been the money guys Barry was dealing with."

"And now Barry and Denise and Glennon are all dead, so Clemens thinks they might come after him? Because of what he knows?"

"That's his concern," says Muñoz.

"You believe all this?"

"I believe a good piece of it, but not the part about Clemens being on the outside of all this looking in. I think he was knee-deep in it."

"So no immunity?"

Muñoz laughs. "Of course not. What's the upside, anyway? He says he doesn't know who the bad guys are or what they're planning."

"And Cardenas, the customs guy?"

He nods. "Thanks for that. Son of a bitch turned his back when a shipment came in. We're going to nail his ass to the wall."

"What was in the shipment?"

He hesitates. "There are things I can't say, but based on where it came from, and some other things we know, it was probably arms."

"What kind?"

"Possibly shoulder-fired missiles."

"Shit," I say, because an entire country in danger brings out the eloquence in me.

But in terms of my immediate job, making sure that Sam is not charged with murder, it's been a good day. This information, when expressed by Muñoz, can only be a positive.

"We need to go over how much of this new stuff you can say in court tomorrow."

"Remember when I told you this meeting was going to be a mixed blessing?" he asks, as my stomach starts to sink. "I can't testify."

"That's bullshit," I say.

He nods. "It is, absolutely. But I have people I have to answer to and an oath I have to uphold. And both of them are telling me I can't speak about these things in court."

I want to argue with him, but the prospect of it is frustrating, because I know he is not making the decision. That means he can't change the decision.

"You are leaving me with no chance."

He nods. "And I'm sorry about that. But there are things happening that are a lot more important than Sam Willis."

Our chance in the preliminary hearing has officially died. Muñoz has kicked it in the teeth and shot it when it hit the ground.

He viewed the news as a mixed blessing, but it's not that at all, at least not in the short term. His reneging on his promise to testify is a disaster by itself.

When I can't truthfully say that if I was the judge I would rule in my side's favor, then I know we're in trouble. And the fact is that if I were Judge Hurdle, based on the current evidence before the court, I would absolutely hold Sam over for trial.

What Muñoz thought was a positive isn't that at all either, at least not for our case. Clemens's story, if even partially true, would be very helpful. It certainly casts doubt on Denise Price's story, gives a motive for someone other than Sam to have murdered Barry, and opens up a sinister, violent world in which other murders have been committed.

But in making the correct decision to refuse Clemens immunity, Muñoz is ensuring that Clemens will never tell his story in a forum in which it can help us. Maybe someday, if he is charged, tried, and convicted, it can be of use to us. But all the while Sam would rot in jail.

A realistic, and potentially deadly, outcome for our case is that this all just goes away. The bad guys back off from whatever they are planning, Clemens doesn't get charged with anything, and nothing new surfaces to get Sam off the hook.

If that happens, then Sam's fate will rest on basically the same evidence as we have seen in the prelim, which is to say he will go away for a very long time. The thought of that literally makes me sick to my stomach.

It's hard for me to root for a national crisis, assassinations or something else, but the absence of that may mean Sam will be convicted of murder. Talk about a lose-lose situation.

I am dreading every aspect of the hearing this morning, but none more than my conversation with Sam before it begins. We go into an anteroom, and I tell him the whole story, leaving out very little.

I've been updating him as we've gone along, so basically all I have to bring him up to speed on is my meeting with Diane Glennon and then the one with Agent Muñoz.

"So he would let someone he knows is innocent spend the rest of his life in jail?"

"I don't think he's looking that far ahead. And I assume he's trying to prevent something that he thinks is worse."

"That stinks."

I nod. "That it does. I'm sorry, Sam. Demanding this hearing was a big mistake."

"But if we didn't have it, I would have been indicted by the grand jury, right?"

"Yes, but then we wouldn't be seen to have failed."

He shakes his head. "The way I see it is we went down punching. I don't blame you, Andy. You did all you could, and I hope you keep on doing it."

It's an incredibly generous thing for him to say, so of course it makes me feel worse. "You can count on that."

We get into the courtroom, and Judge Hurdle tells me to call our next witness. "The defense rests, Your Honor."

Bader does a quick double take and then shows the hint of a smile. There is murmuring in the gallery, probably reflecting their disappointment. They were likely hoping for a big day.

"Agent Muñoz will not be testifying?" Hurdle asks.

"Not at this time."

"There is no other time," Hurdle says and then adds pointedly, "At least not in this hearing."

"I understand that, Your Honor."

There generally are not closing arguments in hearings of this type, though the judge can ask the lawyers to sum up, if they'd like. Hurdle doesn't make that request of us, which is just as well, since there's nothing I could say that might carry the day.

Instead, Hurdle says, "I will take the weekend to review the record and consider my decision. My ruling will be posted on Tuesday."

He slams his gavel down, and the debacle is over.

The phone rings, waking Laurie and me. Laurie picks it up, because it's on her side of the bed.

"Hello?" Then, "He's right here." She hands me the phone. "It's Hilda Mandlebaum."

I grab the phone, now wide awake. "Hilda, I tried to reach you all day yesterday."

"On the Sabbath?"

"Sorry, I wasn't thinking." I notice that it's still dark outside. "What time is it?"

"Five fifteen. Don't worry, I haven't slept past four thirty in twenty years. And Eli's always up before me."

"Did you get what I need?"

"Some of it. Do you want to see it?"

I tell her that I do and ask her to come right over as I'm getting out of bed.

"Did she get it?" Laurie asks.

"Yup. Sabbath's over."

Laurie and I go downstairs, and she puts

on a pot of coffee. Hilda and Eli arrive about ten minutes later. She's carrying a plastic bag filled with something that I have to admit I hope is more of her rugelach.

It isn't, but what she has is even better. It's a list of the phone calls Diane Glennon has made since her husband was murdered. At my request, using techniques that Sam had taught her on a previous case, she has hacked into Diane's phone records.

I believe Mrs. Glennon lied to us when we went to see her. I have a number of reasons for being quite sure of that; what I'm not positive of is why. And though I think I'm right in my theory, it is the why that Sam Willis and maybe a lot of other people are depending on.

"This is everything," Hilda says. "There are thirty-one different numbers, but some of them she called more than once. Here's a list of the numbers she called more than three times."

There are three numbers on that list. One of them was called seven times, one four, and one eight. "Do you have the times the calls were made?"

"Why not?" she says, then finds the right page and hands it to me.

I cross-check the numbers that received multiple calls with the time in the hours after Laurie and I left her house. The three numbers were all called in that time frame.

"Hilda and Eli, I need to know where these numbers are. The landlines should be fairly easy, but these might be cell phone numbers. Do you remember how to do that?"

Hilda looks a little unsure, but Eli is nodding his head as vigorously as Eli can nod, which is sort of hard to detect.

"Eli doesn't forget anything," Hilda says. "When you've been married fifty-eight years, there are some things you want them to forget, but he never does."

Because every cell phone has a GPS device built in, the phone company's computers always know where that phone is, as long as it's turned on. And because of Sam's expert tutelage, if the phone company's computer knows something, then Eli Mandlebaum knows it as well.

"Where are Leon and Morris?" I ask.

"Back at the bunker."

"Today's not Purim or anything, is it?"

"Of course not."

"Good, because I need this right away."

"All of the numbers?"

"Yes, but start with the three that were called often. Hilda, this is important."

She nods, accepting the challenge. "Let's go, Eli."

It's almost six in the evening before Hilda and Eli are back. This time they have Morris and Leon in tow; the Holiday Inn bunker must be unmanned. They've brought with them the locations of the phone numbers that Diane Glennon has recently called.

"Which are the three multiple-call numbers?" I ask.

Hilda points. "Right here. This one is a landline, in Fort Lee; it's a delicatessen. This is also a landline; it's the number for the Paterson Police Department." She had obviously been calling Pete.

"What about the third one?"

"It's a cell phone, but it hasn't moved since we've been watching it."

"Where is it?"

"About thirty miles north of Monticello, New York."

"Is it a residence?"

"It doesn't seem to be anything," she says.

"What does that mean?"

"Eli?" She turns the floor over to Eli, who says that they have information that it used to be a summer camp but closed more than ten years ago.

"And an operating cell phone has been at that location all day?"

"Yes," Eli says.

I send them back to the bunker, with instructions to let me know if the cell phone's location moves. That leaves Laurie and me to try and figure out what our next move should be.

"Andy, whatever they might be planning, that is most likely their base of operations."

"I know."

"Are you going to call Muñoz?" she asks.

"No. You're going to call Marcus."

I simply cannot rely on Muñoz at this point. He has other priorities, and I'm not even saying that he shouldn't. But I have to defend my client, my friend, to the best of my ability. And right now the only way I can do that is by finding out for myself who is on the other end of that phone.

Marcus is at the house in fifteen minutes. Using the Internet, we actually can get an idea of what the camp looks like, or at least what it used to look like. Laurie finds pictures of the place that former campers have nostalgically posted on social media sites, and Google Maps gives us an overhead view, which is no doubt more recent.

The place almost looks like a small army post. Since invading army posts is not a specialty of mine, I let Laurie and Marcus work out a plan for us to execute.

I really need to balance my representation of Sam with the public good, and I come up with a way I think will enable me to do that. I call Muñoz, who is not my favorite person these days, and leave a message that it's an emergency. He calls me right back.

"This is your lucky day," I say.

"Yeah, I've had a whole bunch of those lately. What do you want?"

"What I want is for you to kiss my ass. But what I'm going to do is make you a star."

He doesn't sound thrilled yet. "How are you going to do that?"

"I don't know what the conspiracy is yet, but whatever it is, I'm going to give it to you on a silver platter."

I tell him to get a bunch of agents, including a SWAT team, and have them in Thompson, New York, tomorrow morning at seven o'clock. It's about ten minutes from the campsite.

"What the hell is going on?" he asks.

"You'll know tomorrow morning. I'm going to do something with some friends. If we succeed, or if we don't, you'll be the first to know. Just be ready to move when I call you."

"You'd better not be wasting our time."

"Hey, it's Memorial Day. Either way you can be home for your barbecue."

The drive to the camp location takes about ninety minutes. We take two cars, for no particular reason other than there might be a time when we'd need them. Laurie drives with Marcus, and I go alone. I've found a motel about twenty minutes from the site. There are closer motels, but just in case someone at the site is familiar with me, we want to make sure we're not seen.

I get there at eleven o'clock, rent two rooms, and settle in to wait for Laurie and Marcus. They are going to drive close to the camp, to scout out the area and make any revisions in the plan that are required.

Marcus has night-vision goggles and binoculars. It's good that he does, because the closest I have to that are 3-D glasses that I got when Laurie and I went to see *Avatar.*

I start worrying at about one o'clock in the morning, and by the time the two of them arrive at close to three, I'm a nervous wreck. During that time I question my decision not to just turn this over to the FBI about four hundred times.

The plan is for us to enter the camp at five o'clock, when it's still dark and we hope most of the occupants will be sleeping. That's just two hours away, so the possibility of getting any sleep ourselves is out of the question. Speaking for myself, there is no way I could sleep anyway.

We gather around a table, and Marcus and Laurie draw a layout of the camp as they've now seen it. It's very similar to what we had before, with the notable difference that they think they now know which buildings are occupied.

They are estimating ten people in three buildings, as well as two guards patrolling the perimeter. According to Laurie, patrolling is overstating it; the guards are sitting in chairs, getting up only every twenty to thirty minutes to walk around.

"The key to it all," Laurie says to Marcus, "is for us to eliminate the guards silently. Can you do that?"

"Yunh." He says it casually, as if Laurie has asked him if he could pick up a quart of milk at the grocery store.

"Just so we're clear, 'eliminate' is a euphemism for 'kill'?" I ask.

"It is."

"Any chance we can just knock them unconscious?"

Laurie thinks about that for a moment and says, "It probably increases the risk fivefold to try it."

"You know, I've made some educated guesses here, based on phone calls Diane Glennon made. What if these are guys out fishing, and she was calling her uncle Charlie to find out if he caught any marlin?"

"Marlin in Monticello?" Laurie asks.

"You may not be focusing on my key concern."

"The guards were carrying AK-47s, Andy. This is not a fishing trip. But if you have doubts, now is the time to pull the plug. Because Marcus can't just knock those guys out, and we don't have the time or materials to bind and gag them. Leaving them alive to come up behind us is too dangerous."

I take some time to think about it, going over in my mind why I believe that Diane Glennon was lying to us, and the implications of it. If we're wrong, if I'm wrong, we're in very deep shit.

Not only is it deep shit, it's deep illegal shit. The law has a tendency to frown on those who kill innocent campers.

Of course, even if I'm right, we're not exactly tiptoeing through the tulips. There are probably ten armed and very dangerous people in that camp. We are three people, and one of them is me.

Two against ten usually does not work. Of course, Laurie is a trained police officer, and Marcus is Marcus.

"Let's do it," I say, turning to Marcus. "If you can, knock them out cold. If not, do what you have to do."

We arrive just outside the camp at four fifteen. For us to be successful, we are going to need to know exactly how many people are in there and where they are. Our assumption is they are occupying three buildings, which brings us to the weakness in our plan.

I am going to be responsible for one of those buildings.

But the only way we can get the information we need is for Marcus to go in and thoroughly scout out the area. And the only way he can do that is for him to take out the two guards.

"Good luck," I say.

"Yunh," says Marcus, and he's gone.

For the next thirty minutes, Laurie and I wait, not hearing anything at all except for this really loud drum, which I finally realize is my heartbeat.

I take the silence as a good sign. If Marcus was detected by the bad guys, they would have no reason to react silently; by now all hell would have broken loose. Marcus failing actually isn't the worst thing that could happen; the worst is if he succeeds and it turns out the guards were not actually bad guys.

Suddenly Marcus is there, standing next to us. He was so silent that I had no idea he had arrived, which probably is not a good sign for the two guards.

"We set?" asks Laurie.

"Yunh."

"Were you able to just knock them out?" I ask.

"Nunh."

Oh.

We go over the plan for the last time, based on the information Marcus has accumulated. Fortunately, one of the buildings has only one person in it, and therefore that's the one that will be my responsibility.

We're ready to go, and Laurie kisses me. I've got a hunch she doesn't do so because I'm adorable but rather because it could be the last time we'll ever get to do it.

That would be a shame.

Marcus doesn't kiss me, which is just as well, but he does give me the handgun I'll be using. He had shown me how to use it in the motel — basically just pointing and pulling the trigger. If I have to use it, I may add in some moaning and whimpering, just to jazz it up.

Marcus leads us onto the campgrounds. I almost trip over one of the dead guards and make the mistake of looking at him. His body is pointing north and south, but his neck is east and west. It's a sight I won't soon forget.

We can see the three buildings. There are others farther down the road, but I can only assume, and trust, that Marcus has determined they are empty. If they're not, we've got a problem.

I know which building is mine, but Marcus points it out to me just in case. My overwhelming feeling is fear, on behalf of all of us, but creeping in is a sense of responsibility. I simply cannot screw this up.

I go over in my mind exactly what I'm supposed to do. Marcus and Laurie, while knowing the plan, will probably wind up operating on instinct. I can't do that, because my instinct is to be at home petting Tara.

We get to our respective doors, and the silence is deafening. Marcus had said he believed the doors were unlocked, but he couldn't be sure. He had shown me on the motel door where to shoot the lock if the door wasn't open.

I'm rooting for it to be open.

The buildings that Marcus and Laurie are covering are fairly close together, while mine is set apart some. For that reason there is not going to be a signal to move; I'm to do so when I hear the noise.

And then comes the noise, guns firing and loud shouting. It's magnified, coming against the previous complete silence, and it jars me even though I knew it was coming. I turn the doorknob, and the door opens.

Thank you.

I burst into the room, screaming "HEY! HEY! HEY!" over and over. It doesn't make a lot of sense, but it makes noise, and I'm not going to get graded on content.

I also, as instructed, fire one bullet into the ceiling. It turns out that I am not coordinated enough to shoot and yell "HEY!" simultaneously, but the sound of the shot is so loud that my voice would have been drowned out anyway.

There is enough light from the moonlight coming in through the window that I don't have to search for a light switch. There is a bed, more of a cot, set up across the room, and a man has woken up and is now standing, his eyes trained on me.

It's amazing, but I think something has finally turned out as I expected. If my deductions and suspicions are correct, this is Richard Glennon.

I point the gun at him and say, "Sit back down, Richard. Or this time you will stay dead."

It's not a great line, but it's better than "HEY! HEY! HEY!"

The gun feels like it weighs four hundred pounds. I'm holding it with two hands away from my body, pointing right at Glennon. It's the way I've often seen it done in the movies; I just wish there was a director around to yell, "Cut!"

"No way you'll shoot me," says the man, who has not denied being Glennon.

"From this distance, it would be pretty tough to miss." He must know something I don't, because he seems a hell of a lot more confident than I am.

There are two desks in the room, placed side by side, with three computers and a bunch of files on them. Whatever they were doing, this is command central. I would love to go over there; I've got a feeling that's where the answers are. But I can't take a chance.

"Who were you going to kill?" I ask.

He laughs. "It would be quicker to tell

you who we aren't going to kill."

"It was for the money?"

"Amounts you can't imagine," says Glennon.

"Paid by who?"

"By you. Every time you put gas in your car."

"Foreign terrorists?"

"That's not how they see it. They see it as defending themselves. And if I don't do it for them, someone else will. They'll keep coming."

Where the hell is Laurie or Marcus? I want to get over to that desk, and I want to put this damn gun down.

"You want to get in on the money?" Glennon asks. "It would be the easiest thing in the world."

"Actually, the easiest thing in the world will be putting you in a cell for the rest of your life."

Finally Laurie comes in, pointing her own gun at Glennon.

"Nice work, tough guy," she says to me. "You really know how to handle yourself."

"I could open a law practice in Dodge City." Then, "Meet Richard Glennon."

"So you were right."

"For once."

"You were right about something else,

too," she says. "This was no fishing trip."

"Where are the others?" I ask.

"Marcus."

Enough said.

"Why don't you take him to be with his friends?" I point to the desk. "I'm going to check out that stuff."

Suddenly Glennon lunges at us. I move into a state of frozen panic, but Laurie shoots him in the shoulder, and he hits the ground, moaning.

She keeps the gun pointed at him. "Get up," she says. If she feels guilty about shooting him, she's hiding it well. It's something for me to remember if we ever have any domestic spats.

Laurie leaves with Glennon, and I head over to the desk. It takes about ten seconds for me to have an idea what I'm looking at, so I stop and call Muñoz.

"This better be good," is how he answers the phone.

"You have no idea," I say and quickly tell him where we are. I glance again at the desk while we're talking. "Muñoz, get here as fast as you possibly can. This defines life and death."

It's a ten-minute drive from where Muñoz and the other agents are to the camp, and it takes them seven to get here. In the meantime, I check on the others. Marcus and Laurie have the camp's occupants in one of the buildings, lying side by side on the floor, on their stomachs. Another one is lying on his cot, a large hole in his chest.

I go back to Glennon's room, and I'm there when Muñoz and the others arrive. "What the hell is going on?" he says.

"Richard Glennon is alive," I say and point to the desk. "But if you don't hurry up and deal with this, nobody else will be."

Muñoz goes to the desk and starts looking at the material. "Holy shit," he says.

I couldn't have put it better myself.

He yells out for another agent to come join him, and I leave to find Laurie. The other agents have taken over the job of watching over the bad guys, leaving us with little to do other than hang out.

Within a half hour, what seems like a hundred people arrive, some FBI and some Homeland Security. There are also a couple of ambulances, though Glennon is the only one with any medical issues that need treating. The rest are either unharmed or Marcus has assured that they will never need medical treatment again.

In any case, the camp has more people in it than at any time since parents' visiting weekend. The main focus is on Glennon's building and the material on that desk, but when I attempt to walk back in, two agents block me from doing so.

"Nobody enters this building."

"You've got some nerve," I say. "I invited you guys into this building. I'm the reason you're here. This is my building."

"Not anymore," the agent says.

How quickly they forget.

There is really nothing for us to do here now, and we're probably the only people in the country who don't have a clue what is going on out in the world.

I tell Laurie that she and Marcus should go back home and that I'll call her later. I'm sure we're all going to be questioned intensively about what went on here, but right now nobody seems inclined to do that. They have other things on their plate.

I am not leaving until I talk to Muñoz.

It's another three hours until I see him. A helicopter lands on what must have been the camp baseball field, the third one to do so. For a couple of reasons, I figure it must have some big shots on it. First of all, I don't think small shots travel around on helicopters. Second, Muñoz immediately comes out of the building and walks in that direction to greet them.

I walk up alongside Muñoz and say, "You

forgot to thank me."

He looks at me for a moment and then nods and says, "You did good. Thank you."

"Now it's your turn."

"There are still things more important than Sam Willis."

"No. Right now nothing is more important than Sam Willis."

I get home just as the televised press conference is about to begin. The secretary of
Homeland Security is announcing that a
terrorist plot has been foiled. On the po-
dium with him are the attorney general of
the United States, the FBI director, and
Special Agent Ricardo Muñoz.

I've made Muñoz a goddamn star, and
Sam Willis is sitting in a cell.

The secretary comes right to the point.
There were to have been between fifteen
and twenty assassination attempts on politicians, in conjunction with Memorial Day
festivities. At this moment, all the targeted
individuals are safe, and extra security has
been assigned to them.

In eleven of the cases, the alleged assassins have been apprehended, and the FBI is
actively pursuing the rest. The situation is
fluid, and because the investigation is in its
earliest stages, the department will not be

commenting further at this time.

The media are actually well out in front of the government revelations, as they usually are. Alarm signals went off loud and clear when parades and speeches were suddenly canceled all over the country, and reporters have been digging at the story ever since.

Sources within the FBI had revealed, anonymously, that this was a terrorist reaction to the American practice of targeted killings, mostly by drone strikes, in remote corners of the world. Since the United States does not acknowledge and never comments on this strategy, no one will confirm it on the record.

Laurie and I watch the coverage for a while longer, but it's all becoming a blur to me. I'm exhausted; we got no sleep last night, and I've always found conducting armed invasions of summer camps to be particularly tiring.

"Where does all this leave Sam?" Laurie asks.

"Well, tomorrow Judge Hurdle holds him over for trial. Then we need to see if there's some way we can turn this to our advantage."

"Got any thoughts on that?"

"No, but maybe I will tomorrow. Right

now I've got to get some sleep."

"Today was quite a day," she says.

"Just another day at the office, babe. Just another day at the office."

Twelve hours of sleep leave me more rested but not any smarter. I'm still not sure how the national news will all fall out and how I can use it to benefit Sam.

I'm angry at myself for not coming to the jail yesterday to tell Sam all that has happened; he had a right to know. I meet with him before the court session, and he listens in amazement as I go through it.

"You're like Wyatt Goddamn Earp," he says.

I blow on my finger as if it were a six-shooter. "Somebody's got to keep law and order in these here parts."

He asks a bunch of questions about the conspiracy before getting to his own situation. That's to his credit. If I were he, all I'd care about would be how it will affect my case.

"So who killed Barry?" he asks.

"I would say Denise, but not because of

any marital problems. I think Barry was going to stop the money laundering and maybe even turn state's evidence."

"Why, if it was so profitable?"

"He must have gotten an idea of what the money was ultimately going to buy, which is why he was going to see Susser to confirm it. He got scared; he was a money guy, not a murderer."

"And Denise?"

"She wasn't about to cut down the money tree." I don't get into the obvious fact that Denise was deeper into the operation, because I don't want Sam to realize that his mentioning the "guy in Columbus" to her caused Kyle Austin's death.

"What is going to happen to Mark Clemens?" Sam asks.

"I'm sure he's going down. Muñoz didn't come close to buying that he was an innocent bystander. He was in this up to his eyeballs and is probably the reason that Denise was able to be drawn into it."

"So they were really having an affair?"

"I'm sure they were."

Then he gets to the key question. "How did you know Glennon's wife was lying?"

"Because she wasn't Glennon's wife."

"How could that be?"

"First of all, when we talked to her, she

was going on about how happy her husband had been, and how he had given no indication that anything was wrong. Yet not only had he acted like he was panicking, but he had told me that his wife was scared to death."

"There were a lot of reasons she could have been hiding that from you. Maybe she was still scared they might come after her if she talked."

I nod. "Right. Which is what I first thought. But then she started going on and on about all the close friends they had made in the area, and especially at the company."

"So?"

"So the information you had gathered said he had only been there six months. So I mentioned her husband's boss, but I used a different name and she didn't correct me. None of it was ringing true for me, so I asked her how her husband's children were doing, the ones from his previous marriage. She said they were doing okay."

Sam smiles. "And he didn't have children?"

"He wasn't even married before. But she had no idea about that, because she wasn't really Glennon's wife; she was just someone he was using. A plant. In fact, Glennon isn't even married."

"Why did he have to have a wife?"

"So she could identify his body."

"Who was the dead guy in the car?"

"I'm not sure, and the body was cremated so we may never find out. My guess is that it was the guy referred to as Carter. Glennon and his bosses were cleaning up all loose ends. It was important to Glennon that everybody believe he was one of those loose ends, that he was dead."

"How come?"

"Because when you do something like he was doing, the U.S. government will not rest until they get you, maybe sooner, maybe later. Just ask bin Laden. But if they thought he was dead, there would be no reason to go after him."

"And everybody was in it for the money?"

"Except for the people putting up the money, and possibly some of the others. They think they're doing God's work. Fortunately, they don't have drones to do it with."

Finally, "So where does this leave us?"

"Eventually we're going to win this, Sam. I haven't figured out how yet, but we'll make it work in our favor. If I have to go public with everything, I will."

"But I could be in a cell for a while?"

I'm not going to lie to him. "You could be in a cell for a long while."

It might have been the most successful game of telephone ever played. That venerable children's game consists of one person telling a detailed story to another, who relates it to a third, who relates it to a fourth, and so on. By the time the last person hears the story, it has usually been totally and comically altered.

Of course, it was never previously played on quite this high a level.

In this case, Special Agent Muñoz told it to his boss.

His boss told it to the director of the FBI.

The director of the FBI told it to the U.S. attorney general.

The U.S. attorney general told it to the attorney general of New Jersey.

The attorney general of New Jersey told it directly to Thomas Bader.

Thomas Bader told it to Judge Calvin Hurdle.

And from beginning to end, the story never changed.

As meetings in chambers go, this is a really good one.

"Just so you won't be surprised," the judge says, "here's what's going to happen. We're going to go into court, but I am not going to issue a ruling. Instead, I am going to call on Mr. Bader, and he is going to officially request that all charges against Sam Willis be dismissed."

"Sounds like a plan," I say, relief flooding me. Muñoz has obviously come through.

"Do you have any questions?"

"Yes," I say, standing up. "Can we hurry this up? I don't want Sam to be a prisoner a moment longer than necessary."

I go back into the courtroom, followed by Bader and soon after by Judge Hurdle.

"What's going on?" Sam asks.

I smile. "Enjoy the moment."

And he does. He enjoys the part where the charges are dropped, and he continues to enjoy it as Bader graciously goes on to say that it is the firm belief of the State of New Jersey that Sam Willis is completely innocent of any crime.

When it's over and Judge Hurdle slams down his gavel, Sam asks me, "What happens now?"

"We get the hell out of here."

We go to my house, both to celebrate and so Sam can take Crash home. Amazingly, when Crash sees Sam, he jumps off the couch and runs over to him, tail wagging. It is the greatest single burst of energy he has displayed.

Laurie makes lunch for everyone, though Tara and Crash are again stuck with store-bought biscuits. We make plans to go to Brooklyn tomorrow night to cheer Edna on in the first round of the crossword tournament. Sam's not going to join us; he's taking Hilda and the bunker gang out for an early dinner at the kosher deli in Fair Lawn.

Unfortunately, Laurie tells me that she's rescheduled her trip to Wisconsin, and that she's leaving for a week on Friday. I'm going to be mature about this and trust that she'll come back; I'm certainly not taking on another client to keep her here.

After lunch, Sam is sitting on the couch, petting Crash. "Let Edna win the tournament," Sam says.

"You still think he's good luck?" I ask. "Since you got him, you've been imprisoned by the State of New Jersey."

"He saved my life," Sam says. "And if he hadn't, then you wouldn't have gotten involved in the case. And if you hadn't gotten involved in the case, you know how many people would have died yesterday?"

I think about that for a moment, weighing the logic. Then I walk over and pet Crash on the head. "Any chance you can arrange for the Giants to win the Super Bowl next year?"